Jean-Christophe Rufin is one of the founders of Doctors Without Borders and a former Ambassador of France in Senegal. He has written numerous bestsellers, including *The Abyssinian*, for which he won the Goncourt Prize for a debut novel in 1997. He also won the Goncourt Prize in 2001 for *Brazil Red*. His novels include *The Red Collar* (Europa, 2015), *Checkpoint* (Europa, 2017) and *The Dream Maker* (Europa, 2017).

Alison Anderson's translations for Europa Editions include novels by Sélim Nassib, Amélie Nothomb, and Eric-Emmanuel Schmitt. She is the translator of Muriel Barbery's *The Elegance of the Hedgehog*

THE HANGED MAN
OF CONAKRY

Jean-Christophe Rufin

THE HANGED MAN
OF CONAKRY

*Translated from the French
by Alison Anderson*

Europa
editions

Europa Editions
1 Penn Plaza, Suite 6282
New York, N.Y. 10019
www.europaeditions.com
info@europaeditions.com

Copyright © Flammarion, Paris, 2018
First publication 2022 by Europa Editions

Translation by Alison Anderson
Original title: *Le suspendu de Conakry*
Translation copyright © 2022 by Europa Editions

Library of Congress Cataloging in Publication Data is available
ISBN 978-1-60945-733-4

Rufin, Jean-Christophe
The Hanged Man of Conakry

Book design by Emanuele Ragnisco
www.mekkanografici.com

Cover photo by Robert Pastryk / Pixabay

Prepress by Grafica Punto Print – Rome

THE HANGED MAN OF CONAKRY

I

The crowd was gazing at the hanging body. An unbroken line of Africans—men, women, children—occupied the pier and the entire sea wall all the way to the red buoy marking the entrance to the Conakry marina.

Eyes were trained on the top of the mast. It was high tide, so the hull of the sailboat was almost level with the edge of the dock. The body stood out against the uniformly blue tropical sky. It could be seen from far off. From their balconies in the villas along the waterfront, numerous residents, only just awake, were staring at the horrible sight. Some had taken the time to fetch their binoculars. They could tell that the victim was a white man, attached by one foot. His hands were swollen, and blood was trickling down his scarlet face.

Absolute silence reigned over the docks. All you could hear was the dull rumble of buses along the avenue, in the distance.

The alarm had been sounded at daybreak, which, in these latitudes, occurs all year round at six in the morning. The news spread quickly. Anyone lingering on the beach at that hour—itinerant peddlers, boys playing football, sailors tinkering with their pirogues—had rushed over, not to miss the excitement.

As the sun pulled away from the horizon, it made the smooth surface of the sea sparkle with light. The heat was already intense, and everyone's skin was beginning to drip with sweat. No one dared to speak. They all watched closely: later they would have to remember and tell the others.

The police showed up after twenty minutes or so. But it was a neighborhood patrol, two men in uniform in a creaky old vehicle. Seydou, a sort of caretaker at the marina, had them climb into his skiff and rowed them out to the sailboat. A little later, when the silence was even heavier, the eagerly listening onlookers heard shrill cries coming from the sailboat.

They could see a third figure moving about on deck. As the sailboat was moored some distance from the pier and silhouetted against the sunlight, it was hard to make out what was happening. But among those observing the scene with their hands shading their eyes there were sailors, used to peering out at sun-bright horizons. One of them said that a woman had just appeared on deck. Another one, a short while later, recognized her:

"It's Mame Fatim," he cried.

Almost immediately, a third one added:

"She's stark naked!"

And then, suddenly, the fear that had been silently gripping the crowd since the discovery of the hanging body exploded into nervous mirth. Hundreds of people, standing in rows above the filthy water of the marina, burst into raucous laughter. Those who weren't toward the front laughed, too, without knowing why. They began hopping and shoving to get their share of the spectacle. A woman fell into the water, and two children, who were holding hands to reassure each other, were pushed in after her by the jostling crowd. A few men dived in to rescue the woman, who didn't know how to swim and was flapping her arms about and screaming. The children managed to grab hold of a ladder built into the stone wall of the pier and climbed back up, careful not to slip on the rusty rungs.

Almost at the same moment, a group of officials, including higher-ranked police officers, had arrived on the clubhouse terrace and were walking down the sandy path toward the docks. Seydou had come back with his skiff, and now he rowed the newcomers two at a time out to the scene of the incident.

The woman on the deck of the sailboat had been hastily wrapped in a sheet that one of the policemen had found in the cabins. She was waiting by the bow, sitting on a sail locker. The deck was very crowded now, and the newcomers did not look comfortable. They were holding on as best they could to the stays of the mast. Then one of the police officers gave an order, and a few policemen began to busy themselves by the rigging, releasing the halyards one by one. Suddenly, the corpse, hanging by one foot from the mainsail halyard, came crashing to the deck, bashing one of the officials as it fell. He could be seen holding his head, and for a long moment no one paid any attention to the body; everyone was focused on the man in the three-piece suit who'd been struck by the dead man as he came tumbling down.

The sirens of ambulances and police cars wailed as they approached through the streets behind the waterfront. Traffic was dense so early in the morning. It took a while before the flashing lights cast their blue reflection on the trunks of the palm trees along the drive to the marina. In the meantime, the figures on the sailboat had turned away from the winded official; he had come round and was sitting by the helm, rubbing his head.

Two policemen escorted the woman, still wrapped in her sheet, to the skiff. She was a rather plump, fairly light-skinned young African woman. Her hair was disheveled, and her face was twisted with sobs. The buzz of voices grew louder when the small boat docked in front of the clubhouse.

"Mame Fatim . . . that's her, all right," the crowd whispered.

No one was laughing anymore.

The woman climbed into an ambulance, which disappeared, sirens wailing.

It took longer to bring the dead man across. The skiff

wasn't big enough. They had to use a Zodiac for which the marina manager had the key, though he'd never driven it. Once the corpse was disembarked, everyone could confirm that it was a tall European man with thick gray hair. Most of the people, while they didn't know him, had already seen him on the beach in recent months. Everyone knew that he had taken Mame Fatim on board a few weeks earlier.

He was dressed in lightweight white canvas trousers and a pale blue flowered shirt. When the two policemen lifted the body out of the Zodiac and laid it on its back on the cement pier, the crowd let out a cry: the man's chest was bright red. A long, bloody wound had gouged a veritable crater in the victim's chest. A policeman hastily covered the body with a sheet. It soaked up the blood, and before long all you could see, on the shapeless mass, was a brown spot spreading ever wider. Two ambulance workers immediately took the corpse away.

The Guinean policemen continued the investigation on board, bending over as they hunted for clues. A French customs official also came to inspect the sailboat.

The crowd, having had its fill of morbid sights, began to disperse, commenting on what they'd seen.

* * *

It was noon when the driver left Aurel, a member of the consular service of the Embassy of France, at the entrance to the marina. Although he was short and fine-boned, it took him considerable effort to emerge from the car. It was a two-door Clio, the service's most basic, dilapidated vehicle, the only one that his boss, the consul general, would allow him to use. Aurel acted as if it were a huge sedan: he would fold the passenger seat forward and sit in the rear, which was really only intended for a small child. He inhabited the space in a dignified manner, with his knees level with his chin and his head touching the

ceiling. He alighted from the car with the same air of importance. After all, "Severus" was one of the titles given to Roman
emperors, as was "Felix," actually. Aurel had never forgotten
that particular history lesson: dignity, like happiness, is an attrib-
ute of sovereignty. Every one of us can grab our share, if we so
desire. Dignified and happy, the consul headed toward the clubhouse, a row of royal palms on each side standing to attention.

It was difficult to determine just how old he was. In spite of
his bald pate, circled by a crown of salt-and-pepper curls, his
facial expressions were almost youthful. But his clothes gave
him the bearing of an old man. His usual work outfit consisted
of a pinstriped suit with three buttons, a shirt with a pointed
collar, tinged yellow here and there from endless washings, and
a red-and-green striped necktie. Whenever he went out, he
wore a long double-breasted tweed coat with wide lapels,
which he kept carefully buttoned. As a protest against the
unjust fate that had exiled him to this African capital, he made
it a point of honor never to deviate from his usual sartorial
habits. He dressed as he would have for the middle of winter
in his native Romania or, at a push, in France, his adoptive
homeland: Paris, to be precise. Fortunately, he did not sweat.

When he crossed the terrace in this outfit and entered the
clubhouse, all conversation ceased. The curious onlookers had
left. Only the regulars were still there, leaning against the bar,
with the marina manager and one of the Guinean policemen
standing guard to make sure there was no looting at the sailboat crime scene.

Aurel took in the little group in a glance. With the exception of the African, all the others were white, over fifty, and
potbellied, their eyes shining with drink. They wore Hawaiian
shirts they'd hardly bothered to button and, below that, swim
trunks or shorts. Most of them had flip-flops on their feet or
went barefoot in old boat shoes.

When they saw this curious, bundled-up little character

standing by the picture window that gave onto the terrace, the men lounging at the bar counter sat up straight. One or two of them buttoned their shirts or slipped on the shoes they'd taken off when climbing onto the barstools.

Aurel was well-acquainted with their reaction. He knew he had come very close in his life to being a person of authority. Unfortunately, there was some indefinable element missing: the first impression he made never lasted. It was immediately followed by ironic smiles and shrugs.

Aurel had never set foot in the yacht club. And yet, after their initial surprise, everyone had recognized him. The marina manager winked at the men around him. Someone chuckled. Two or three men, to look serious and give an impression of composure, began assiduously sipping their drinks.

"I gather the consul general is on vacation?" asked Ravigot, the manager.

Aurel knew that his superior, Baudry, consul general of France in Conakry, was a member of the club, although to the best of his knowledge the man had no sailing experience. It was simply an opportunity for him to drink together with joyful company, to hear local gossip and tell a few good stories. The one about Aurel, to start—the catastrophic deputy posted to his consulate. "A Romanian, can you imagine, and with a dreadful accent. He's such a disaster that you can't trust him with anything. I stuck him in a closet. Literally. Without a telephone or a computer. Wondering why he hasn't been let go? It's not for lack of trying. Every boss he's had has tried to get rid of him, myself included. But, unfortunately, he's a government employee with lifelong tenure."

"What a pain!" Ravigot had belched. He used to run a car repair service in Bayeux and swore only by free enterprise.

"It's not that simple," another regular had objected, a retired natural sciences teacher, who occasionally went out fishing on a small boat without ever catching anything.

All the windows in the bar were open. Gusts of warm air wafted up from the docks, carrying smells of rotten fruit and the tide.

"Come in, come in, Monsieur le Consul," said Ravigot.

The manager, like all the expatriates, was familiar with the subtle hierarchy of embassies. He pronounced the word "consul" in an off-hand manner that made it fairly clear he was on familiar terms with the other, real, consul "general."

"Thank you."

Aurel approached the bar as solemnly as possible. But it was already too late, their minds were made up. Everyone was smiling as they watched him hurry over with his coat flapping around his ankles. The closer he came, the more apparent his short stature. Normality had changed sides, after a brief spell in Aurel's favor. Once again, what seemed natural was to be almost naked, or wearing a ridiculous flowered shirt, slumped over one's glass of Ricard and smelling of sweat. Aurel had not expected anything different.

Once in front of the bar, he hunted in his coat pocket and took out a bundle of business cards. He handed one to Ravigot. He affected nonchalance while he waited for the reaction, placing between his teeth an amber cigarette holder with a filter-less Camel wedged into it.

Ravigot read his card attentively. Under the red, white, and blue logo of the Ministry of Foreign Affairs was his name, Aurel Timescu, and his title, "Consul de France." Ravigot was a tall fellow, and age had made him heavy with fat, but his face remained rugged, furrowed with wrinkles. He was very good at acting indignant. And while his displays of rage might impress newcomers, the regulars would double over with laughter. He handed the card to the former teacher, and it was passed around.

"Look at this, you lot. And try to mind your manners around Monsieur le Consul."

You had to know Ravigot well to see that, beneath his bushy brows, his eyes were shining with a naughty, ironic twinkle.

"And what can we do for you, Monsieur Timescu?"

"Tell me about the dead man."

"Mayères?"

"Is that his name?"

Aurel had taken out a notebook in fake leather and was scribbling in it with a little silver pencil.

"Yes. Jacques Mayères. Actually, what can I offer you, Monsieur le Consul?"

"Do you have white wine?"

White wine was one of Aurel's weaknesses, something Baudry had lost no time in describing. "He drinks like a fish," he asserted. "Obviously he has to keep busy in his closet . . ." But Aurel's passion for white wine was another story his superior knew nothing about: Tokaji wine, the vineyards of central Europe, a great nostalgia for the lands where, in his opinion, despicable barbarity mingled with the most refined civilization.

"No, unfortunately not. I can offer you beer, red wine, or soda."

"Then nothing, thank you. Did you know the deceased well?"

"Did we know him? Well actually, only yesterday he was sitting where you are now, leaning against the bar counter, and most of these gentlemen saw him."

The little gathering mumbled in agreement.

"Had he been staying in your marina for a while?"

"Almost six months. It's February now; he got here at the end of the wintering period, in September."

"I imagine he showed you his papers when he got here?"

Ravigot did not merely run the bar. He was in charge of the yacht club, and every newly arrived crew had to check in with him. He then went on to inform the police and customs if the boat came from abroad.

"He showed them to me, naturally."

"And did you keep photocopies?"

Ravigot smiled and picked up his glass. He emptied in one go what was left of his pastis.

"You know, we don't stand on ceremony here. We trust people. He was a regular guy, you could see that. And anyway, all the time he's been here, there's been no trouble."

"So you didn't keep his papers."

Ravigot rubbed the back of his neck. His hand came back full of sweat.

"Are you sure you wouldn't like to make yourself more comfortable?" he urged. "We're among friends here."

Aurel ignored his question.

"Maybe the Guinean authorities kept a copy of his documents?"

"The Guinean authorities!" echoed Ravigot, looking around him, eliciting a few smiles. "Oh, I'm sure they did. You know what their administration's like . . . a model of order and discipline!"

Aurel lowered his eyes and looked at his shoes. Oiled with polish year-round, they were now covered in sand from the path. They looked like breaded cutlets. He sighed and reached for his notebook.

"Do you recall how old he was?"

"Sixty-six. I know because he was born in August, like me. A Leo, the best sign! Three days more, and we'd have been exactly five years apart."

"Did he tell you what he used to do?"

"That's all he ever did. You know what retired people are like. Well, you're too young, but you'll find out."

This was Ravigot's petty revenge on those patrons who, day in day out, must have bored him senseless at the bar with memories of their working life.

"He had a business in Haute-Savoie."

"In what branch?"

"You hit the nail on the head! Wood, that was his branch . . ."

Ravigot's bad joke brought smiles back to the regulars' faces.

"His father, or his grandfather, I'm not sure anymore, had founded a little sawmill. He began working there when he was sixteen. When he inherited the place, he expanded. By the end, it was the biggest in the region. He controlled the entire industry, from the purchase of standing timber right down to furniture manufacture. And his exports went as far as Saudi Arabia."

"Do you know what happened to his business?"

"He sold it. To the Chinese, if I'm not mistaken. He got a bundle for it."

"Any children?"

"No, actually. He said he was free."

"Never married?"

"That wasn't something he really talked about."

"Yes it was," interrupted one of the clients. "He told me he had a wife back in France."

"Did he have a lot of money with him?"

"He must have had quite a lot in reserve on the boat. He paid everything in cash. He often had five-hundred-euro notes that he didn't even bother to change into CFA francs."

Aurel scrupulously wrote everything down. Ravigot had already refilled people's glasses twice. Time was passing. Everyone was getting hungry. The interrogation was beginning to seem a bit long.

"Is it consular information you're looking for?"

Aurel got flustered. As far as the consulate was concerned, all he needed was the victim's personal information. And he'd let himself get sidetracked. Ravigot had no way of knowing that in a former life Aurel had wanted to work for the police. He never got over not being able to conduct investigations. It was a missed calling for him. He would have been able to put his psychological and observational skills to use, as well as his chess player's rigor. He was convinced he would have been a genius at it. Whenever he could, Aurel liked to carry out his own investigation, separate from the police and for his benefit alone. It was basically a hobby, but he had to keep it secret and not arouse any suspicion.

"I won't keep you any longer," he said, ironically, because that was precisely what he wanted, to go on with his questions a little longer. "The girl who was on board, do you know her? Did she come here with him?"

And so that he wouldn't seem to be shirking his consular duties, he added:

"Is she French?"

"French! Mame Fatim? She wishes she were, and she's tried everything she could."

There was some derisive laughter. A few of the clients looked down. Aurel gathered they had all known the young woman, and probably in a biblical sense.

"Mayères didn't marry her?"

"He might've done, if it had gone on like that," said the retired teacher. "But when it came to that sort of thing—all due respect to the deceased—he was a real moron."

Ravigot knocked a few glasses together, and Aurel sensed it was meant as a distraction. He had cast a dark look at the old teacher.

"This is all very well," said Ravigot, glancing at the massive black and yellow diving watch on his hairy wrist. "I have to go and check the weather. And the Brits are expecting me on board for lunch."

Aurel had been roundly dismissed. He closed his notebook and took his leave of the company. No one moved, except him. He walked slowly to the terrace, avoiding the wicker armchairs with their blue-and-white striped cushions. Two ceiling fans churned the humid air and stirred up a nauseating mix smelling of dead fish and sweating bodies. Once he reached the French doors that opened onto the terrace, he paused for a moment. That was enough for him to get a view of everything. The clubhouse was set at a certain height, but you couldn't see the entire marina from the terrace. Apart from the sailboat involved in the incident, there were only four other sailboats moored there. One of them must belong to a family, because women's and children's clothing was drying on the rigging or lying in the sun on the warm deck. All these boats were close together, but Mayères's was anchored a long way from them, in the opposite corner of the marina.

Aurel also observed that a number of little boats and dinghies were tied up along the pier, most of which probably never got used.

"You have a very pleasant establishment here," he said, straight out, turning back to Ravigot.

He also knew very well the effect this would have—that of unsettling people who had lavishly made fun of him, by giving himself a flamboyant departure, so totally unexpected that it was downright worrying.

"In a private capacity, I like this place very much. I'll be back."

Aurel said this in such a majestic tone that those who heard him were left speechless.

Before immersing himself in the pool of sunshine flooding the terrace, he reached into his pocket for a pair of dark glasses. They were a model specifically designed for use on glaciers that he'd found in a sporting goods store in France. Leather blinders on the side completely blocked out the light. Thus protected from the outside world, Aurel set off down the sandy path that led to the exit, trying not to think about his poor shoes.

urel went straight back to the embassy. He hated the way they smiled at him, the gendarmes guarding the entrance gate. It was always the same old rigamarole. His driver was a wrinkled old Guinean who had lived through colonization and the dark days of Sékou Touré, and the little white Clio didn't look like an official vehicle. Unlike the big dark sedans belonging to the ambassador and the consul general, the Clio's arrival didn't elicit a hurried opening of the gate. A gendarme came out, cautiously approached, and leaned in the driver's window.

"Oh, it's you, Mohamadou," he said, recognizing the driver.

Then he noticed Aurel, squeezed into the back seat, and greeted him.

"Oh, Monsieur le Consul! Forgive me. I didn't see you."

All this accompanied by a smile that spoke volumes. Then the gendarme parsimoniously opened only one side of the gate, and the car had to make its way through the narrow opening. Aurel didn't care; he'd seen worse. By force of circumstance, life had left him inexhaustibly impervious to far more humiliating vexations. He had grown up in Ceaușescu's Romania, which had been an exceptionally rigorous school in that respect, arming its graduates permanently against stupidity and scorn.

The Clio dropped him off outside the consular building, but Aurel decided not to go in right away. He walked across the main courtyard. Four gardeners were busy tending a lawn decorated with little flower beds. A sprinkler offered a touch of coolness. He walked around the chancery and went down four steps to the police cooperation service. A Guinean duty officer greeted him respectfully. Aurel was grateful to him. He felt that Africans typically showed him greater regard. He preferred not to give this a racial explanation. It wasn't because he was white, or because whites often still aroused a sort of fear inherited from the brutal days of colonization. He was convinced that Africans placed a special emphasis, perhaps of a magical nature, on the *spirit* of the people they met. Aurel liked to think they respected him because they sensed he had a pure and generous soul.

"Is Commissaire Dupertuis in his office?" he asked the duty officer.

"Yes, Monsieur le Consul."

"Alone?"

"He's with Commissaire Babacar Bâ."

"May I see him?"

"I'll let him know."

The duty officer picked up the telephone.

"He'll see you now, Monsieur le Consul."

Aurel went down the familiar corridor. Of all the department heads in the Embassy, Commissaire Dupertuis was the only one who behaved in a friendly manner toward him. It's true that Aurel had turned on the charm where he was concerned. They found out they shared a passion for crime novels, and Aurel had turned him on to lesser-known works. Above all, he had demonstrated his talents as a pianist for Dupertuis. When the commissaire gave a party at his house for his fiftieth birthday, Aurel agreed to play all evening long. He went through his entire café-concert repertory. The guests were delighted. Aurel only started drinking at around eleven in the evening. When they'd had to evacuate him, dead drunk, at two in the morning, there was hardly anyone left and no one noticed.

Dupertuis was sitting in front of his desk, his Guinean colleague across from him in a leather armchair. The commissaire was a plump man. His smooth face, with his glowing pink skin, evoked a good nature and the cunning of a peasant brought up in the open air. He was a native of Saint-Jean-d'Angély, a town he often spoke of as if it were a capital on the decline; he himself seemed to have preserved, beneath his coarse exterior and despite his modest background, an almost aristocratic refinement.

"Come in, Aurel. What a pleasure! Are you filling in for Baudry while he's on vacation?"

"I don't know yet. But I went to the marina to take down the consular information."

"A strange business, don't you think? Bâ and I were just talking about it. He's in charge of the investigation. We're in Guinea, I have no criminal investigation powers here; the case is under the jurisdiction of the Guinean police. Isn't that right, Babacar?"

The commissaire was obviously eager to show the degree to which he respected African sovereignty.

"Do you have any information about the victim?" Aurel asked cautiously.

"I get the impression he knew quite a few people here."

"That's strange for a tourist. Do you know who he was seeing?"

"Mainly people with boats. For example, the husband of the ambassador's secretary. One of our gendarmes, as well, the one who used to win dinghy sailing competitions in France. Several guys from the trade delegation. And no doubt plenty of others. People have been calling me to ask for news ever since they heard . . ."

"But I don't think he was registered at the consulate."

Aurel had called from the car using the driver's cell phone: he didn't have one himself, for the sake of preserving his peace

and quiet. Arlette, who was in charge of the database of registered French residents, had grudgingly and hastily checked her
files.

"You know what these sailors are like," moaned the commissaire. "They don't view themselves as residents."

Aurel sighed, with the desolate air he used to assume in the
presence of officials in communist-era Romania, when he was
unsure of his interlocutor's opinion.

"When you got here, Bâ was just telling me what they found
at the crime scene. Go on, Babacar."

The Guinean glanced nervously at Aurel.

"You can speak in his presence. Aurel is a trusted friend.
And he often has good ideas."

Aurel smiled, inclining his head. It was true that Dupertuis
liked to consult him about his investigations. This was the fruit
of a long labor of getting to know him, which had started with
their discussions about noir thrillers and had gradually drifted
toward real affairs the policeman was dealing with.

"As I was telling you," continued Commissaire Bâ, "the
Frenchman was killed by a high-caliber bullet fired at point-
blank range, right into the chest. There was a safe in one of the
cabins, and it seemed to have been easily forced open. It was a
fairly basic model. We found no money or items of value in it."

"And the girl?"

"She says she was raped. They found her at the bow of the
boat, gagged with masking tape, with her hands and feet
bound."

"Did she see her aggressors?"

"She says there were two or three of them. She seems to
have everything rather confused."

"Were they white or African?"

"She couldn't describe them. She says she was asleep in the
bow of the boat, and to wake her up they started kicking her.
They were hooded, and it was pitch black out."

"That's true, there was no moon last night," Aurel confirmed discreetly.

"She wasn't sleeping in the same cabin as this . . . Mayères?" asked Dupertuis.

"Who knows. She'd been living on his boat for several weeks. But as to what they did together . . ."

"You told me people at the yacht club know her well?"

"Yes, and what's more, we've had our eye on her for a while. We have a little file on all the girls who hang around there. She's a Serer who was born in Senegal, in the peanut region. Her parents were small farmers. They were ruined by the fall in prices. When she was five, she came with her family to the slums on the edge of Conakry. She left school very early. After trying her luck at various odd jobs, she began hanging out in bars. One of her girlfriends supposedly brought her to the marina for the first time, and she started living off the passing sailors. The girlfriend actually married an Austrian and left for Europe. It's safe to assume that Mame Fatim had the same agenda."

"The people on the other boats didn't notice, didn't hear anything last night?" asked Dupertuis.

"We haven't finished questioning them. But apparently no one has anything to add."

"Are there many sailboats in the marina just now?"

"Four. Two retired English couples. They were on land the night of the murder."

"Doing what?"

"A photo safari, inland. We have sufficient evidence."

"And the others?"

"An American family with children. Nothing suspicious, at first glance. We're looking into it. And the last boat belongs to a single Italian man. That one, we've got doubts about. He has a fair amount of influence here, and as far as we know, his alibi is rock-solid."

"Which means?"

"A woman."

Bâ seemed somewhat embarrassed to be speaking in Aurel's presence. The commissaire encouraged him with a nod.

"A minister's daughter. Not something to go shouting from the rooftop. But all the staff saw her."

Which meant they turned a blind eye. Among policemen, they knew how these things went. Some information had to be handled discreetly.

"So, in short," concluded Dupertuis, "nothing pointing to the boats."

"There is the fact that Mayères's boat was moored some distance from the others," ventured Aurel, without arousing any interest.

"And the manager of the marina, does he sleep there?"

"He has a bungalow in the back, at the edge of the avenue. With the sound of taxis and trucks passing all night long . . ."

"Was the victim's cell phone found?"

"No, it must have fallen in the water at the time of the crime."

"That's a pity," said Dupertuis, and, as he never lost an opportunity to emphasize the local police's lack of means, he added: "We won't go dredging the bottom of the marina for that. That's what we would have done in France. I just don't think we have the technical means to do that here . . ."

He got up and went to stand behind his desk. Aurel had noticed when they were talking together that the commissaire liked to strike a canny sleuth pose before suggesting a theory. If he were completely honest, Aurel would have to admit that Dupertuis's deductions were generally pretty naive, to say the least. But the policeman expressed them in a learned manner and was always careful to connect them to an episode in his training. That way he made sure his authority was unassailable. Aurel always had to use cunning to set forth his own ideas because, more often than not, they reduced the commissaire's peremptory conclusions to dust.

To prevent his facial expressions from betraying his thoughts, he took out his cigarette holder and began chewing on it. Dupertuis motioned to him to light up. Aurel took two or three acrid puffs that hid his face completely.

"In the end, your case seems fairly straightforward to me, my dear Bâ," Dupertuis began, in his learned manner. "Cases of this type are legion, and the training manuals are full of them: a perfect example of the felony murder. A rich old white man. He's been here six months, he spends lavishly and visibly, people notice, and one day, they board his boat. The only question is whether the girl is a victim, as she claims to be, or whether she's the one who tipped them off. Was she really raped?"

"We sent her to the hospital to be examined. What we can say is that she had the marks of a beating on her face and that her hands and feet were bound so tightly they bled."

"That doesn't prove anything," said Dupertuis, sitting down at his desk. "So, how can we help you?"

"I don't know yet. If I need some technical support, I'll let you know."

"We're always here for you, my friend."

"Thank you. In the meantime, we've mobilized all our informants to try and find a lead. If it's local thugs who were behind it, we'll hear something fairly soon."

"Keep an eye out for any five-hundred-euro notes," suggested Aurel. "Apparently his safe was full of them."

"How do you know that?"

Aurel coughed as if some residue of stale tobacco lingering in the amber tube had poisoned him.

"Well, the manager at the marina told me."

Dupertuis raised one suspicious eyebrow and stared at the little consul.

"And was there, in your opinion, anything else in the safe—jewelry, gold, deeds?"

"I'll try to find out. I have to call his family, and his lawyer."

Commissaire Bâ's telephone sounded with the ringtone of the call to prayer. He answered and spoke for a long time in Pular. During the conversation, Dupertuis talked quietly with Aurel.

"In the end, it's not as interesting as I'd hoped. As usual around here, it's a pretty basic affair."

Dupertuis sincerely liked Africa and had true friendships with his Guinean colleagues. It would have shocked him had someone told him that he spoke about them with a condescension not fully free of colonial undertones.

"You do agree with me, don't you, Aurel?"

He always put this question to him with a touch of concern in his voice. Never knowing where Aurel got his strange ideas from, the commissaire waited uneasily for him to point out some detail that would jam the perfect workings of his theories. It was the same when they played chess, and he preferred not to play with him for that very reason.

"I totally agree, yes," said Aurel.

There was nothing for it: the more he initially seemed to approve, the more his objections would come as a shock later and make his initial attitude seem like deceit. Might as well come straight out with it. Aurel took a deep breath and added, "But . . . what I don't understand is why, if this is a crime about money, they went to the trouble of hoisting the body to the top of the mast."

Dupertuis registered the blow. At first he sat there with his mouth open and his eyes staring vacantly. Then he sat up straight and pulled on the sides of his jacket.

"That's just the way it is, pal. Criminals are not normal people. They have ludicrous ideas."

He refrained from adding, "Like you." Aurel smiled humbly,

like a valet who has just been struck by a stick and admits he deserved it.

After leaving Dupertuis's over-air-conditioned office, Aurel went through his daily ordeal: after the main courtyard—still rather cool, thanks to the shade of the central palm tree and the freshly watered lawn—he walked along the burning ground of the path leading to the consulate. The walkways of the building, once a military hospital, were open onto the exterior. The damp air accumulated in these narrow passageways, heating up the tiles and the paint, which over the years had turned the color of baked flour. Aurel wedged a new cigarette into the amber tube and lit it. He relaxed, as if the burning smoke somehow cooled the air. He didn't bother to go to his closet. He knew what he had to do. Continuing along the passageway on the ground floor, he went straight to the visa section.

This was the engine room of the consulate. The place was lined with files, and a dozen haggard people with shadows under their eyes were busy at the counter or hidden away in offices piled high with paperwork. Aurel viewed the visa section as an illustration of hell and above all of absurdity. In an atmosphere of jostling and irritation, the game consisted in asking those Africans who were determined to go to France for a quantity of useless documents that they were then obliged most often to purchase at top dollar from counterfeiters. Devoured by the visa section, this continuous mass of paper was chewed, digested, absorbed, and evacuated in the form of stamps to be applied—or not—to their passports. When someone was denied their visa, the process of appeal generated even more paper. Everyone ended up getting into France eventually, with or without a visa. The only end result of this labyrinthine system was the fabrication of disgruntled applicants and exhausted staff.

The head of this satanic outpost was called Lemenêtrier. He

was a civil servant nearing the end of his career, and it was obvious at first glance that he would not make it to retirement. His face, with its grayish-brown complexion, was like some administrative form a deranged user might have filled out haphazardly, leaving big wrinkles, spots, and marks everywhere. He was a widower, and rumor had it in the embassy that he resorted to the services of very young African prostitutes, some of whom were even underage. This suspected vice had earned him a hefty file that for years had compromised any hopes he might entertain of promotion.

Baudry, the consul general, like any good civil servant, knew how to recognize and appreciate manifestations of voluntary slavery, so he had placed his trust in Lemenêtrier. Whenever he went on vacation, he left Lemenêtrier in charge of the consulate. According to strict administrative logic, that role should have fallen to Aurel, who was slightly higher in rank.

By going to see Lemenêtrier, Aurel knew what he was doing. He found him, as usual, hunched over a pile of files. He was studying them, holding his glasses between the thumb and the index finger of his left hand, while his right hand held the only weapon he had ever touched: a red ballpoint pen. He sniffed when he saw Aurel come in, because this was a tic of his, as if anything unpleasant were immediately transformed into a bad smell.

"Morning, Bernard."

"Yes, Aurel. What are you doing here? Do you need a visa?"

This was a joke that Baudry had popularized in the consulate, one of those tiny vexations reserved for needling Aurel. A particularly elegant reference to his foreign origins. Aurel would react with painful impassivity, pinched lips and eyes lowered, to the delight of the consul general. Lemenêtrier now repeated the joke, unsmiling, as a simple ritual to reassert his allegiance to his boss.

"I went to the marina this morning on consular business."

"Why the marina?"

"There's been a crime. A Frenchman was murdered."

In his fishbowl, Lemenêtrier was always the last to be informed.

"How did you hear about it?"

"By chance."

Which was true. When Aurel had arrived at the embassy that morning, he had happened upon a young Guinean policeman Bâ had sent with a message for Baudry. Aurel had taken possession of the letter, insisting he would make sure it was handed to the right person, and, naturally, he had opened it. Bâ had scribbled a few notes summing up the first findings on the boat. Aurel had taken advantage of the godsend. Criminal issues were virtually the only thing in life that could still excite him. He had rushed to the marina.

"I'm going to monitor the case," he announced emphatically.

Lemenêtrier, staring at Aurel, tightened his fingers over his glasses and made them vibrate on his nose, as if he were adjusting the focus. He played for time by motioning to Aurel to put out his cigarette. Then he resumed his indifferent expression.

"So?"

"So I need a computer with an internet connection. And a telephone with an outside line, too. I have some research to do in order to contact the family."

This was a reasonable request, but it did contravene Baudry's orders. The simplest way to resolve the dilemma would be to call the consul general, wherever he was on vacation. But he was traveling around Spain, and, to save money, he had switched off his cell phone. Lemenêtrier had already tried to reach him the day before regarding a sensitive visa issue, with no luck. According to the pecking order, the head of the visa section did not have the authority to refuse anything Aurel might request. And he did not trust his own skill in handling procedure. Better to let him have his way.

"All right, we'll set that up for you."

"Right away."

"Right away."

"One more thing: Hassan, the young guy who's in charge of the mail, will be under my orders for the duration of the . . . procedure."

He had almost said investigation, but fortunately caught himself in time.

Lemenêtrier didn't answer, leaving the future open. He didn't object, because he didn't have the power to, but no one could say he had formally approved.

"Have a nice day," he muttered, and, after this long interruption in his regular breathing pattern, he re-immersed himself in his file, to fill his lungs with bureaucratic oxygen.

Aurel hurried to his closet, calling Hassan on the way. Less than an hour later the young employee, with his long bony arms and smiling nonchalance, showed up with a computer terminal he'd unearthed, which he hooked up, turned on, connected to the internet, and linked to the collective printer on the landing. Then he went down to the switchboard to link the telephone to the outside line. Aurel, fired up by the job at hand, even went so far as to remove his jacket and loosen his tie. He raised the blinds over the single window in his closet because it looked out on the passageway; ordinarily, he didn't want anyone to see him sleeping, reading, or composing music. The rumor that something was going on with him quickly spread through the building. Several secretaries walked past his office on various pretexts, astonished to see the door open and the blinds raised. They would have to get used to it.

Aurel was very skilled when it came to computers. To ensure he'd be left alone at the office, he had pretended to be the type that knew nothing about them. But in fact, given the right personal motivation, he could transform himself into an accomplished geek. The computer keyboard thrilled him just as much as that of the piano; when he placed his hands on it, he was filled with an exuberant joy.

As soon as Hassan had set up the device, Aurel began tapping away and in record time had obtained a wealth of information regarding the victim.

The much-lamented Mayères had certainly not felt similarly at home on a computer. He had no Facebook page and had hardly left any direct traces on the web. However, his career had been public enough, and various websites still recalled some of his activities. *Le Dauphiné* newspaper had published several articles about him: when he had been awarded the Order of Merit, for example, or when he sold his business to the Chinese. He had lived in Seynod, not far from Annecy, where he was something of a local notable. Aurel didn't waste time reading all these documents. He bookmarked them in a file he called "Marina." At this stage, the only thing he was looking for was a picture. He couldn't find any satisfactory ones: they were always full-length pictures of Mayères in a group, taken from a distance. He kept on looking. He found some more valuable information. The contact details and name of his wife, for example, a reference to a deceased brother and a sister who was a doctor, married to a lawyer in Lyon, but who went by her maiden name. He found the husband's professional telephone number quite easily, as well as that of a doctor's office where a certain Jocelyne Mayères was one of the associates. Aurel checked his watch. He hadn't seen the time go by, but it was already late afternoon. Because of the time difference with France that time of year, it would be too late to get anyone at work. He continued his internet searches. Night was falling quickly over Conakry. Hassan was walking up and down the corridor, and Aurel realized that he was waiting for permission to leave. He lived very far away, and with the evening traffic jams, it would take him a good two hours to get home. Aurel told him he could go.

3 4 · JEAN-CHRISTOPHE RUFIN

"I'll lock up my office."

For the first time the word office, instead of closet, had sprung to his mind. It was a sign. A short while later, the gendarmes came to inspect the phenomenon for themselves and were astonished: Aurel doing overtime. He merely gratified them with a distracted grunt and went on chewing on his cigarette holder. Because, for the last few minutes, he'd been following a lead. At last, at around nine o'clock, he found what he had nearly given up on: a close-up photograph of Mayères. It was over fifteen years old. He found it in an employee directory on the page of the Chamber of Commerce and Industry of Haute-Savoie, where Mayères had briefly been in a position of responsibility. Aurel enlarged it, reframed it, and touched it up slightly to make it less blurry. Finally, he printed it out on the collective printer, after switching it back on. Mayères had a square face, sharp features, a long, slightly crooked nose, and thick eyebrows. It looked like a facial composite portrait, with the same robotic features—expressionless, hard, impenetrable, neither cheerful nor sad, humorless and emotionless. The face of a man fired up for action, yet withdrawn on a personal level. Aurel did not take the time to study the portrait in detail. He merely slipped the print-out into a cardboard folder. Feverishly, he put on his jacket and coat, locked the office, left the building, and pattered home, hugging his precious document.

He lived in a little villa two hundred yards from the embassy. It had been engulfed by a garden that neither Aurel nor his predecessors were in the habit of tending. There must have been a lawn somewhere once. It had been overtaken by branches drooping from the trees and swamped by bushes overflowing from their beds. Clusters of purple bougainvillea blocked the windows on the ground floor and caused a permanent darkness to reign in the interior. Aurel liked this sepulchral atmosphere.

Baudry had interpreted this lifestyle as further proof of his subordinate's stinginess. True, Aurel was saving on the cost of a gardener. But it was a consequence and not the cause of his decision. The truth was that in these gloomy rooms, their windows invaded by vegetation, he completely forgot he was in Africa. The moment he got home, thanks to his furniture and his books, he was back in a Central European ambiance. A Central Europe influenced by Paris, but the Paris he had dreamed of when, as an adolescent, he was subjected to the ugliness of communism. The heart of this Mitteleuropa home was the piano, which had gone with him every time he moved. The advantage of the Ministry of Foreign Affairs, it must be said, was that it put up with and even financed this sort of capricious behavior. Wherever he went, and he had already been posted to several very distant locations, his instrument, duly enveloped in felt blankets, followed along in a container.

It was an upright, with a metallic sound and no particular charm, and was desperately in need of tuning. Two of the bone keys were chipped. To be honest, it was more of a café-concert piano than a concert one. That's what Aurel liked about it. Two copper candle-holders above the keyboard meant he could play by candlelight alone.

The moment he got home that evening, Aurel took off his overcoat and suit, removed his tie, and opened his shirt. With his shirt-tails floating over his bony buttocks, he sat down at the piano. He took the photo of Mayères from his file and placed it on the music stand.

Then he cracked his knuckles, lifted the heavy keyboard lid, and removed the felt cover. Staring deep into the eyes of the deceased man, whom he was basically seeing for the first time, he played the opening bars of "Mack the Knife" and other airs by Kurt Weill.

He played late into the night, his teeth clenched on the amber tube, never taking his eyes off the dead man.

III

I'd like to speak to Dr. Jocelyne Mayères, please."

The problem, as always, was his accent. With his voice that tended to croak, and the way he rolled his "r"s, and this intonation of his, like some Danube peasant's, Aurel knew it would be difficult to announce himself to a stranger over the telephone using his title "consul of France." It would sound like a practical joke, and more than once people had indeed hung up on him.

"Speaking."

Better not make any effort to sound like a Parisian. Aurel had already tried, and the end result was a sort of meowing that disintegrated into spluttering.

"My name is Aurel Timescu," he said, pronouncing his name the Romanian way. "I'm the French consul in Conakry."

A long silence followed that he didn't know how to interpret.

"Go on, I'm listening," the woman on the other end said finally.

"It's regarding your brother, Monsieur Jacques Mayères."

Still just silence.

"Well . . . there's been an accident . . . I mean, we're not sure yet, actually . . . he was found this morning on his boat . . . He was . . . dead."

"He was murdered."

Her voice was clear, confident, and her words were not a question.

"That is . . . probably. But what makes you say that? Did he mention any particular danger or threat?"

"What time are the flights from Paris to Conakry?"

"There's an Air France flight in the early evening."

"Fine. I'll get the TGV from Lyon-Part-Dieu, and I'll be on that flight."

"Wait, we can speak for a moment. I have a few questions for you."

"We'll talk when I get there. I have a lot of practical things to deal with before leaving."

"Give me your cell phone number, at least. I'll call you this evening to see whether you managed to make the flight, and I'll meet you tomorrow morning at the airport. You won't have time to apply for a visa. I'll have to help you get one on arrival."

"That would be great. Thank you."

Aurel wrote down her number in his notebook.

"Just one question. Was your brother married?"

"We'll talk about it when I get there."

"I have to contact his wife."

"She lives in Hyères. They were separated."

"Is it a Maître Hochard who sees to their legal affairs?"

"He's their lawyer, yes. Now, please, I must go. We'll talk about all that tomorrow morning when I get there."

Aurel hung up, then sat for a long moment imprinting the woman's voice on his memory. He was as sensitive to sound as he was to image, although each had the gift of evoking different things in him. When he listened to *The Threepenny Opera* or looked at a painting by Klimt, it was the same era that came to him, but the tonality was very different. Similarly, when he heard the sister's voice, while looking at the photo of her deceased brother, it seemed to him he was entering the same house but through different doors. Brother and sister had a similar authority, an equally hard façade. They must both be decisive and stubborn, traits that could point to a brutal side . . . But behind the tough appearance, perhaps the sister shared the sensitivity he suspected in the brother. He would have a better idea once he met her.

Next, he left a message at the law offices of Maître Hochard, who was "on an outside call" all morning. Judging from the assistant's tone of voice, Aurel got the impression that the lawyer was not particularly assiduous. From what he'd read about him on the internet, Hochard was well into his sixties. He must be starting to slow down. Moreover, the assistant had offered to put Aurel through to a clerk, who was probably the one who did all the work. He declined her offer, preferring to speak to the lawyer himself.

These calls had taken a good part of the morning. Aurel decided to head out for lunch. The idea had come to him during the night, while he tossed and turned in his bed, to go and have a sniff round at Fall's, perfectly casually. Knowing he would be in for a particularly busy day, where he would have to remain as discreet as possible, he didn't take his usual overcoat, just a putty-colored trench, cinched at the waist with a belt. Only Aurel could possibly imagine such a garment could make him invisible in Conakry in the middle of the hot season.

In his ongoing concern to remain relatively camouflaged, he did not ask to use the consular Clio but simply flagged down an ordinary taxi in the street. It was an ageless Fiat, decorated with red plastic seat covers and religious trinkets: stickers celebrating the Virgin, keychains with effigies of St. Christopher, and rosaries dangling from the rearview mirror. These divine protections were in no way superfluous, given the condition of the steering, the tires, and the brakes. The car drove slowly along the coast road then headed down a little dirt track where deep ruts had formed during the rainy season. All the way at the end, between two garage entrances, was the narrow passage you had to go down on foot to reach Fall's. Aurel paid the taxi driver (too much, but it would have been beneath his position to haggle) and walked on to the restaurant. You could already hear the sea close by, breaking against the rocks. In the cinder-block passageway, the sound was amplified, almost terrifyingly so: the continuous roar of the waves was followed by a dramatic hiss as they broke on the shore. Two small boys were playing football with a ball made of rags. Absorbed by their game, they bumped into Aurel, without apologizing.

On emerging from the passageway, Aurel was in the restaurant itself. It consisted of a reed-covered terrace that went right down to sea. Below the terrace, the water, trapped beneath concrete piles, made a muffled sound. On the side facing the sea, the stone wall had been made slightly higher to prevent the stronger waves from splattering the nearby tables.

It had just struck noon, and only two lone diners were having lunch. Aurel had come here only once, upon his arrival. Baudry had actually shelled out on an invitation to dinner, not so much to be polite as to be able to say, later on, that he'd given Aurel an unbiased welcome and, at the same time, emphasize his lack of gratitude. He had taken him to Fall's so it wouldn't cost him a fortune.

Fall, the boss, who had given his name to the establishment, was busy in the kitchen. A young waitress, wearing a short, tight dress, sat Aurel at a bad table in the passageway, near the entrance and far from the sea. The place was renowned for its staff, hired by Fall himself on the basis of very particular criteria: he took only young, pretty women, whose bearing and smile and attitude would allow his patrons to hope for favors the women weren't authorized to offer, at least not while they were working. The clientele consisted primarily of expats. You would look in vain for families with children, who preferred the restaurants at the major hotels, with swimming pools and playgrounds to keep the kiddiwinks occupied, and above all where husbands wouldn't be distracted by generous rumps and protruding breasts.

The place mainly attracted single men on their own or in a group, sometimes using the pretext that these were "business luncheons" for an excuse to hang out with their own kind. Baudry was a regular. In the end, they were the same kind of patrons as those who loafed around the marina clubhouse, and that was what interested Aurel.

Fall had a memory for faces. It was a business asset of prime importance to him. People like to be called by name, to be recognized. For the solitary individuals who made up the bulk of his clientele, it was particularly agreeable to feel pampered, like family. Fall immediately recognized Aurel because he had seen him several months earlier together with the consul general. It was perfectly possible, too, that Baudry had entertained him, as he did everyone, with the escapades of his subordinate. In any case, with his usual overcoat, his welder's sunglasses, and his cigarette holder clenched between his teeth, Aurel Timescu rarely went unnoticed. Fall put down his cloth and came out into the restaurant to greet him.

"How are you, Monsieur le Consul? This is an honor!"

Fall was a Susu originally from the south of the country. He was well padded, and when he was cooking, he delighted in tasting the dishes. Before and after each service, he had his chef make up generous samples for him of everything on the menu. He had round, darting eyes and a fleshy lower lip that he tended to exaggerate, knowing that it gave him a comical and ingenuous look that white people found reassuring.

"Do you have a minute, Fall?"

"Naturally, Monsieur le Consul."

"Sit down, please."

Given Aurel's reputation for being odd, the invitation unsettled the restaurateur somewhat. But he had too much respect for authority to refuse.

"Do you know a certain Mayères?"

"Yes!" exclaimed Fall, wiping his hands on his white apron. "I just heard the news. It's terrible."

"Terrible, indeed. Did he come here often?"

"Well, mainly at the beginning. When he first got here, he made his meals on his boat, but you know what it's like. From time to time, you feel like getting out and seeing people."

"Women?"

Fall wrinkled his nose. He didn't like for his establishment to be taken for a brothel.

"In all likelihood."

"Did he have ordinary girlfriends, or did he hire the services of professionals?"

When he heard the word "professionals," Fall decided it was time to react.

"I have no idea. There are no 'professionals' here."

"He might have brought someone."

"Most of the time he came on his own."

"And his last girlfriend?"

"I don't know anything about her."

Fall saw two customers come in, regulars, and he greeted them with a big smile. He turned back to Aurel, allowing his temper to show.

"It's not kind to tease me, Monsieur le Consul. You already know everything. And I have work to do . . ."

"I know what everyone knows. He was found on the boat with a girl, and it looked like she'd been living with him for some time. Do you know her?"

"Vaguely."

"Mame Fatim, does that ring a bell?"

"Ah! Yes . . . Mame Fatim," Fall said distractedly, anxious to attend to his serious patrons.

Aurel rolled his cigarette holder between his fingers and shot him a look typical of an American actor who made a great impression on him when he was young. But this pose, which should have made him interesting, left Fall completely indifferent. There were times when Aurel wished he were tall and strong, to intimidate people. Instead, he constantly had to resort to cunning.

"Look," he hissed, casting a pleading look at the restaurateur, "I won't take much of your time, but I need to know more about this girl. There is quite a lot of money at stake."

Whenever he heard the word "money," whether it meant his own or others', Fall always pricked up his ears. If there was money at stake, it meant they were now in the realm of what he referred to as "serious things."

"Did he leave a packet?"

"Might have done."

"What do you want to know?"

"What you can tell me about that girl," Aurel insisted. "Did she work here?"

For a poor girl who wanted to mix with whites, Fall's restaurant was a reasonably logical step.

"Not long."

"When was it?"

"Last year, just after the wintering."

"Did she leave of her own accord, or did you let her go?"

"A bit of both. She crossed the line, and she knew what to expect."

"Meaning what?"

"She got her claws into a Dutch guy, a regular."

"Because the others . . . ?" Aurel asked, jerking his chin toward the other waitresses.

"The other girls are discreet. But she went right out and carried on in public. She even came to dinner with him here one time, like a client. So I told her she would have to look elsewhere for work."

"And that's when she left for the marina."

"Not right away. First she lived off the Dutch guy. He was an engineer. He was sent here for the renovation of the dam."

"Married?"

"Of course. Once she understood he wasn't going to leave his wife, she took what she could and moved on. That's the way it is, here, for these girls who have nothing. And time is not on their side."

The restaurant was gradually beginning to fill up, and Fall was again casting desperate glances out at the room. Suddenly, he had an idea of how to get rid of Aurel.

"If you like, I'll send for Aminata. They were good friends."

Not waiting for Aurel's answer, he stood up and hurried off to the kitchen. Before long, a waitress appeared, and Aurel invited her to sit down.

"I can't. My tables . . ."

"Don't worry. Anyway, it was Fall himself who sent you over."

Aminata was a slender young girl with fine features. She had combed her hair back into a tight chignon above a very long neck, which gave her a doe-like allure. At the same time, her eyes were cold: it took her only a moment to size Aurel up. He sensed that she had instantly pigeonholed him in the category of pathetic losers.

"You are well acquainted with Mame Fatim, I believe?"

She gave him a sidelong look, and he saw her shudder. A jealous lover? she wondered. Could Mame Fatim really stoop so low? Her answer came cautiously.

"A little."

"I . . . I'm interested in her, you see. What can you tell me about her?"

"I haven't seen her in a while."

Apparently, Aminata knew nothing about the Mayères murder.

"You haven't heard from her at all lately?"

Aurel seemed very interested: he was nervous and feverish, and the girl looked at him with surprise. In her world, they were used to thinking in terms of seduction and desire. She was sure this sucker was love-struck. There was often trouble with men in love who got ditched and then tried by every means possible to get back at the woman who had dumped them.

"No," Aminata said, fluttering her eyelashes. "I just ran into her boyfriend maybe ten days or so ago. He lives in my neighborhood."

"Her boyfriend?"

She'd wanted to do her friend a favor by mentioning the existence of this boyfriend. If Aurel was a jilted lover, it might calm him down. She misread his expression and took for disappointment what was above all profound surprise.

"She has a boyfriend? You mean a fiancé?"

The girl smiled, somewhat spitefully.

"You could put it like that."

"What's his name?"

"Lamine."

"He's Guinean?"

"Yes, why?"

The girl was visibly still enjoying Aurel's confusion.

"This is very important, what you're telling me. This Lamine guy, is he *still* her boyfriend? Didn't you know she was living with a Frenchman on his sailboat?"

"No, I didn't know."

"And where can I find this Lamine?"

At this question, Aminata started to feel frightened. What if this nobody was about to make a fuss? Maybe he wanted to go and settle a score with Lamine. She could already picture the scene.

"I don't know where he lives," she said quickly.

Her haste and flustered air made Aurel realize there must

be a misunderstanding. He sensed she was about to seize the first pretext that came along to rush away. And so he staked his all. He took a business card from his pocket and scribbled his cell phone number on it. The title "Consul of France" always had an effect. It was cowardly of him, he knew. All these girls dreamt of leaving, and the huge problem for them was the sacrosanct Schengen visa. By revealing that he was a consul, Aurel suddenly became incredibly interesting. Any worth he lacked in his person was acquired through his position. The girl looked up from the business card and gratified him with a smile full of promise. As a result, now it was Aurel's turn to feel unsettled. He focused quickly on the conversation to hide his awkwardness.

"Mame Fatim is in prison. She needs help. I *want* to help her."

"In prison?"

"The Frenchman she was living with was murdered this morning. She is a suspect. I have to speak to her boyfriend."

This was a lot of information, and the young woman seemed upset. All she retained of the conversation was that she could be of assistance to a French consul. She would be able to remind him of the fact when the time came.

"He lives out past the airport. You know where the village of Yoff is?"

"Of course."

It was one of the suburbs of Conakry, fairly modest, and it was often used as a hideout for criminals.

"There's an Ethiopian restaurant. Just one, it's easy to find. Lamine's apartment is across the street on the second floor."

"Do you know his last name?"

"Touré."

"Thank you," said Aurel.

He put his hand on the waitress's slender wrist and gave a squeeze. He felt his eyes fill with tears. He'd always wished he

could get rid of this stupid emotional side, but there was nothing for it. Aminata smiled modestly, looking up at him through
lowered eyelashes, both shy and sensual, a look that brought
her success with her clients. But Aurel, far from responding in
kind, removed his hand and took out a handkerchief to wipe
his eyes. She told herself that he was definitely a strange bird,
probably not completely normal. She even began to regret
sharing information with him. Anyway, it was too late now. She
went back to work.

Aurel immersed himself in the menu and ordered a few
grilled sardines, sprinkled with lemon juice and served with
pink rice.

While Aurel was eating, Fall was careful not to go near him.
Nor was it Aminata who served him, but another waitress with
an inscrutable expression.

Aurel used the time to think about the case. Looking at the
tables around him, he tried to imagine Mayères sitting there.
There was a man he could see from behind, having lunch with
an African woman. Aurel wondered whether Mayères had
deliberately chosen this part of the world, and had enjoyed
being here, or whether other reasons had kept him in Conakry,
in spite of himself. What charms did life here have to offer?
Sunshine all year round, yes, but for Aurel this was not a plus.
On the contrary, he liked seasons and would never have sacri-
ficed three of them to live in perpetual summer. The sea? It's
the place where everything ends, where the rock of mountains,
eroded by time, comes to finish its race in grains of sand. Isn't
that what Mayères had done, leaving behind the peaks of his
native Haute-Savoie to end up on this shore? What was his
state of mind? Should one picture him as happy? Or rather,
having seen it all before, had he succumbed to the scheming of
a girl who—and he must have known it—was only after his
money?

Above all, there was this one detail that continued to

puzzle Aurel: why had Mayères been strung up at the top of his mast?

He asked for the bill and climbed into a taxi, still haunted by the image.

Back at work, Aurel found Hassan busy in his office. He had answered the phone in his absence and had just finished speaking with the lawyer, Hochard.

"Did you give him the news?"

"No need. He already knew."

"Through the sister?"

"Yes."

"I'll call him back. Do you have his direct line?"

Aurel removed his trench coat. He'd come up the stairs four at a time, and whiffs of grilled sardine made him fear indigestion. Normally he would have taken an hour-long nap. But the excitement of the investigation had him in its grip, and he immediately picked up the phone.

"Maître Hochard?"

"Speaking."

"Aurel Timescu, consul of France in Conakry."

"Thank you for returning my call, Monsieur le Consul. What a terrible business! Can you fill me in?"

All the lawyer knew was that Mayères was dead, but he didn't know the circumstances. Aurel summed it up for him.

"It's awful, awful!"

Hochard's voice was that of someone who is not at all well. He breathed noisily, and his sentences were frequently interrupted by fits of coughing.

"Had you known him long?"

"Jacques? All my life. I was a friend of his older brother's. We were in school together in Seynod."

"So he went on to entrust you with his affairs?"

"Right from the start. I watched him build his career. His parents were of very modest origins and had a tough life.

Jacques got his start in the tiny family sawmill. Then, when he inherited it, he made it grow and grow. It became a very big concern, of international scope. As for me, I moved to Lyon. It wasn't very practical for him, but he never wanted to hire another lawyer."

"Were you involved in the sale of his business?"

"Along with others. For matters like that, there are usually quite a few attorneys involved. The buyers had their own counsel. Jacques hired another lawyer, and there was also a consultant. But I was associated with everything."

"It must have represented a huge sum of money."

"Huge indeed."

"Forgive me for asking, but what I wonder, given the fact that the buyers were Chinese—"

"Chinese, yes, from the People's Republic. A huge company from the north, from Dalian, formerly known as Port Arthur."

"So my question is: was it all paid for . . . in France?"

For a very long spell, Aurel heard nothing more on the line. He thought the lawyer must be mute with indignation. In fact, he couldn't breathe for laughing. A few gurgling sounds and a series of laborious spitting coughs marked his return to seriousness.

"Excuse me. You made me choke."

"What was so funny?"

"It's just that . . . you didn't know Jacques, of course. Otherwise you would never have asked such a question."

Hochard was still out of breath. He was inhaling deeply to calm himself down.

"You see, Monsieur le Consul, Jacques Mayères was a patriot—but that word isn't strong enough. In addition, it's ambiguous. You might think I'm referring to politics. In fact, he was no reactionary nationalist; he was even, rather, on the left. A left-wing company boss, do you see what I mean? We didn't agree about things like that . . ."

While he was listening, Aurel had pulled up Mayères' photograph on his computer screen.

"But, on top of all that, he was crazy about France. For him, France was more than just a country. It was more, even, than a religion. He loved France the way you love a woman. Though that's not a good comparison for him, either. I'm not sure he ever really loved a woman."

"And yet," Aurel objected, "he sold his business to Chinese people."

"He did indeed! With a heavy heart, I can assure you. He looked everywhere for a buyer. But there's the crisis, and in France these days no one wants to make that kind of investment. Particularly as—like I told you—he was a generous boss: his employees were well paid. Too well paid, according to some. What's more, the Chinese, who had promised they would keep everyone on, immediately forced nearly half the workers into early retirement or out the door into unemployment. It made Jacques sick to his stomach."

"So he was fully paid, in France."

"Everything. And he paid a fortune in tax. It was as if he was proud of it. He never said how much he sold the company for, but he told everyone the amount he had coughed up for the public purse."

"And how much, in your opinion, did he make from the sale?"

"I'm not at liberty to say. Professional secrecy."

"An order of magnitude?"

"Several tens of millions of euros."

"Tell me, Maître, I have been led to understand that he was married?"

"He still is. He and his wife haven't lived together for ages, but they're still married."

"What sort of settlement?"

"Joint ownership of property."

"Are they separated?"

"In practice, but not legally."

"So his wife inherits the lot?"

"You tell me, Monsieur le Consul, how much will go to her."

"What do you mean?"

"After Jacques sold his business, he didn't leave anything in France. He has a measly account with the Crédit Agricole, for which I have power of attorney—wait, let me check, I have the latest statement. In it there is . . . €12,359."

"Where's the rest?"

"He took it with him."

Aurel, who had been tipping back in his chair, almost fell over.

"What did you say?"

"You heard me: Mayères went off with all his money. Everything he had left after buying his boat and making a few charitable donations. He gave his wife the wherewithal to buy an apartment on the Côte d'Azur, since that's where she prefers to live. And then he left."

"Which means that on his boat he was transporting several tens of millions of euros?"

"I fear that is so."

During the silence that followed, Aurel stared at Mayères's face on the screen. He suddenly saw a new expression there. Behind the hard, fixed gaze there shone a cunning little gleam, like a flicker of a smile. Not a social smile, not an anonymous smile meant for everyone; it was, rather, an inner smile, ironic and even sad, a way of judging life and drawing one's conclusions. Oddly, Aurel got the impression that the smile was meant for him personally, as if he were a criminal winking at his accomplice.

"Hello? Are you still there, Monsieur le Consul?"

Aurel passed his hand over his face.

"Yes, yes, forgive me. I was thinking."

"You seem to be upset by the news."

"You probably haven't been told that the safe on board the boat was forced opened and emptied."

"No!"

It was the lawyer's turn to take in what he'd just heard.

"Just after the money, then?" he said tonelessly.

"That's what we think."

And yet, at that very moment, Aurel was thinking of something very different: the body hoisted up the mast.

After a long silence, he began to speak, his toner livelier.

"I imagine you'll be taking care of the succession."

"It won't take long if there's nothing left."

"His only heir is the wife, if I've understood correctly. The family is quite small. They didn't have any children?"

"Yes, they did. Very late, actually, and with difficulty. Aimée had several miscarriages. She had to undergo treatment. In the end they had a daughter called Cléo."

"What has become of her?"

"It's the saddest thing. When she was nineteen, she got into drugs. Heroin, AIDS. She went through a terrible ordeal. Two years ago, she died of an overdose."

"I see," said Aurel soberly; he didn't like thinking about such tragedies, for fear he might burst into tears. "So, to get back to the succession, you can confirm that only his wife is left?"

"His wife and his sister, whom you spoke to and who is arriving tomorrow. But over the years, Jacques made decisions that ultimately meant his wife would be his only heir."

"Have you informed her?"

"Not yet. I'm going to send her an email."

"She doesn't have a phone?"

"She does, but I don't particularly want to speak to her."

"Why not?"

The lawyer seemed embarrassed. He hesitated.

"It's just that . . . quite often, when people separate . . . you know how it goes . . ."

"You mean to say you've chosen sides."

"Oh, 'chosen' is not the right word. To be honest, I never felt like I had a choice to begin with. My friend was Jacques. She—"

"What's she like?"

"Do you mind if I don't answer that question?"

"But I'm going to have to call her myself."

"Well then," concluded the lawyer sharply, "you'll find out for yourself."

IV

Time, in Aurel's house, had come to a deliberate stand-
still in the first half of the twentieth century. It was a
world of dreams. He could, for example, spend hours
staring at a class picture featuring his maternal grandfather,
Rabbi Kahen, with his pupils at the Jewish school in Timisoara.
Aurel looked at each one of the children, who must all have
passed away by now or been very old, and he imagined their
lives. Sometimes it was his extended family on his father's side
that he looked at, gathered around the priest for a Catholic
feast day. His father had been a mailman, the eighth of twelve
siblings. Every year, he went to the countryside near Brasov
and dutifully joined in the major family reunion held in late
autumn. Aurel did not know most of these peasant faces, but
he never tired of peering at their rough features. In the end, his
spirit swollen with all these lives, he would sit down at the
piano. He played for hours to drain the emotional edema
which otherwise would have flowed from him in tears.

From the moment he took on the case of the murder at the
marina, Aurel had been impervious to any other emotion. But
his aptitude for daydreaming, like a muscle exercised by sport,
gave great power to his evocations of Jacques Mayères and the
little world that was beginning to take shape around him.
However, for his imagination to be fully operative, the photograph of the deceased man was not enough. He had to siphon
a bit more fuel from reality. This was why he went on with his
internet searches at home, on his personal computer.

He began with Mayères's wife. He planned on calling her the next day at the earliest suitable time. He did not think she would be an early riser. But first he wanted to find out a bit more about her, since the lawyer hadn't wanted to tell him anything.

According to the records sent by the Office of Vital Statistics at the town hall in Seynod, on June 1, 1969, Jacques Mayères had married Mademoiselle Aimée Agathe Camille Delachat, born October 5, 1949. As Aurel went on with his research he found several families in Seynod by the name of Delachat, most probably interrelated as cousins. One branch of the family had given its name to a sizable public works company. They had overseen several major projects, like the hospital in Annecy or the construction of infrastructure for the Winter Olympics in Albertville.

In 1969, when Mayères and his fiancée were wed, he was nineteen, and she was twenty. Aurel attached great significance to the age at which people got married. To him, it cast light on an essential element of their personality. For men who'd had considerable professional success in life, this criterion made it possible to determine two distinct categories. There were those who focused solely on their work and only thought of getting married once they had made their fortune. One could safely assume that the men in this category found the energy to act and the will to change their condition within themselves. Whereas others, like Mayères, married very young and shared their years of striving and social advancement with their spouse. From there to assuming that their desire for success was not theirs alone, but was also inspired by their spouse, was a step one could not always take. But the question did arise, regardless.

Where Mayères was concerned, Aurel thought the latter assumption suited him fairly well. The clever, hard-working businessman hadn't just found his tender side late in life. If he had given himself, body and soul, to this Mame Fatim, it was surely because for many years he'd already had a tendency to devote himself to a woman. Aurel looked at him and tried to see the features of the nineteen-year-old Mayères. This was something he usually did the other way around, gazing at photographs of children and trying to guess what sort of adults they had become.

He went to fetch a bottle of Tokaji and drank almost half of it in one go. Then he sat down at the piano, still facing Mayères's photo. He let his inspiration guide him and was astonished to hear melodies by Satie emerge from the keyboard. In the rather sorrowful chaos of the *Gymnopédies*, Mayères's features were pared away. Lit only by candlelight, his wrinkles vanished, his hair seemed thicker . . . he was nineteen years old. He was a kid crushed by an authoritarian father, a youngest child to whom too little attention had been paid. One evening at a dance he met a girl slightly older than himself. She was an only child, and her parents must have spoiled her. And then . . . Aurel stared at the portrait, and his mind took him far away. He tried out different theories and checked to see if they matched the face—still enigmatic, although it was beginning to seem familiar.

Aurel needed a smoke. He had been chewing so hard on his amber cigarette holder that there was a hole in it. He went to get another and chose one made of Bakelite and ivory that he had bought in Istanbul many years earlier. He placed a filterless cigarette in the holder, lit it, and grimaced as he inhaled, because it tasted of cold cigarette holder. He washed away the acridity with a long swallow of white wine and returned to his daydreaming.

When he let his mind wander like this, he didn't see the time go by. He fell asleep without realizing. It was already midmorning when he awoke, lying in his underwear on the sofa next to the piano. Two empties of Tokaji lay on the floor. He swallowed a tablet for his headache, then went to make some coffee, got dressed, and hurried to the consulate. He had promised Mayères's sister that he would pick her up at the airport. The plane arrived at noon. He still had a little time. He asked Hassan to bring him an espresso from the visa department. This required negotiating with one of the assistants who collected the money for the capsules. Hassan, with his big eyes and smile, was better at this than he was.

Then he laid out his battle plan for the day. Which also included Hassan: he would send him on the trail of the notorious Lamine, Mame Fatim's boyfriend. In Guinean circles, it was better to call on local people for local snooping. Aurel knew that the presence of a *toubab*, a white man, always excited the neighborhood children. He was in danger of being immediately surrounded by clusters of children shouting, "Money! Pens! Candy!" and so on.

Hassan came back with the coffee. Aurel gave him his instructions and advised him to set off right away. As for Aurel himself, before questioning the sister, he had to stop off to see the commissaire to check on the official investigation. The policeman was reading his mail. Aurel peered around the open doorway.

"The victim's sister will be here soon to organize the funeral," he announced.

"Aurel! Come in, my friend. The sister is coming? I'd like to question her. Would you bring her to me?"

"Naturally, Commissaire. Making progress?"

"Slowly. It turns out the girl was lying. She wasn't raped, and she certainly knows a lot more than she's prepared to say. The Guineans are pressuring all their informants to look for leads."

"Still on the assumption that it was for the money?"

"Of course, what else would it be?"

At chess, too, the commissaire was always optimistic.

"Say, Aurel. They say you've landed on your feet with this case. So you're interested in successions?"

"It's more fun than visas. You have to track down family members, get in touch with lawyers, all that sort of stuff."

"Well, I'm glad for you. I've always thought it was a pity that a young man with your talents was hanging around doing nothing."

It was true that Dupertuis had been almost the only one to defend him. When Baudry had made him the laughingstock of the embassy, the policeman had shown Aurel respect. And whatever else he might think of him, Aurel did not forget that. When emotions like this came to him, he could feel his eyes going moist. He very nearly burst into tears. He grabbed Dupertuis's hand and squeezed it in both of his, a lump in his throat.

"Thank you, Commissaire," he managed to say.

He had meant to ask the policeman for permission to borrow one of the cars from his service to fetch Jocelyne Mayères: he would have made a better impression in a four-door sedan. But in the end, his stupid emotions had prevented him from speaking, and so he headed out to the airport in the back seat of the Clio.

The road went past brand-new, gleaming white villas that testified to the city's recent expansion. The nouveaux riches were exhibiting their abysmally poor taste in architecture. Pediments and colonnades flourished everywhere, but to no purpose at all, tacked on to modern façades. The sunlight annihilated all this, and the proximity of the ocean made the landscape quite lovely in spite of everything. But Aurel could not appreciate it. The absence of clouds, the harshness of the light, the strange vegetation filled him with irrepressible sadness. There are people who break down crying when they hear certain joyful melodies. He knew a professor in Romania who had an epileptic seizure whenever anyone played "La Marseillaise" anywhere near him. To Aurel, this was exactly the same thing. He was disabled, in a way: the heat, the sea, and the bright colors threw him into the deepest melancholy.

To protect himself, he hunted in his pocket for his glacier sunglasses and feverishly put them on. The thick lenses allowed only the greenish outlines of things to filter through; the spectacle became bearable.

The airport was dilapidated and the movement of passengers anything but orderly. Clusters of people amassed at every door, blocking corridors and cluttering the hall with mountains of luggage. Aurel was used to crowds. He had grown up in a disorganized country where you had to stand in line for everything. What was hard for him was to preserve his dignity and determination in such an environment. His gut reaction in a crowd was to relapse into the submissive, passive attitude that the communist world had required of its subjects. But now he had to preserve his sense of initiative, elbow and shove his way through the multitude, flash his papers at the authorities. To overcome his inhibitions, he decided it was preferable to keep his dark glasses on. So it was in near-total darkness that he began making his way forward, pushing past women, bumping into suitcases, shoving children. All around him shouts and insults greeted his passage. And yet, the audacity of this blind man with his eyes screened by dark glasses, charging full speed through the crowd, caused surprise, fear, and, in the end, respect. And it meant that everyone stepped aside and he managed to get through.

He made his way to the arrival gate for the Paris flight. A Guinean duty policeman was blocking the way. Aurel waved his diplomatic badge in his face and was allowed into the area reserved for passengers. The baggage was being delivered, and passengers were waiting around the carousel. The strangest assortment of luggage was going around on the conveyor belt. Not only were there brand-new suitcases with their luxury

logos, but also laundry powder boxes bound in masking tape
or held together with old string.

Aurel spotted Jocelyne Mayères easily, from her appearance
alone. The resemblance with her brother stemmed more from
her expression than her features. She had short, undyed hair.
Her height gave her a sporty elegance, and the years, far from
depriving her face of its youthful features, had added an air of
kindly indifference, as if experience had handed her the key to
life's most important secrets. Aurel recognized in her the type
of woman for whom he immediately felt total admiration, both
paralyzing and delightful. He walked up and greeted her:

"Madame Mayères, I presume?"

She had no idea what Aurel looked like. For a moment she
stared with stupor at this little man cinched into his raincoat,
hidden behind a pair of glacier sunglasses.

"Aurel Timescu, consul of France," he shouted, to drown
out the noise of the crowd.

He handed her a business card. Then he removed his sunglasses, revealing a pair of shy little eyes that made her smile.

Leaving the airport was a long, drawn-out procedure. They
had to negotiate to obtain her visa. Aurel had to call the commissaire to have him confer with his Guinean colleagues.
Finally they were able to climb into the Clio. Madame Mayères
sat in front. She apologized for letting Aurel squeeze in
behind, never imagining that this was his usual spot.

"Have you ever been to Conakry?"

"Never. To be honest, I don't know Africa at all."

Aurel very nearly said, "Neither do I."

"I booked a room over the internet, at the Radisson. Do
you know it?"

"Of course, it's one of the biggest hotels in town. We'll take
you there. You'll be able to drop off your suitcase and freshen
up."

The Radisson had opened only recently. It was located on

the waterfront in a new neighborhood. Aurel, who had never set foot there, took a moment to walk around while Jocelyne Mayères was settling into her room. The building was made all of glass, the architecture very modern and fairly austere; the large, spacious lobby was furnished with gigantic, quite lovely chandeliers. The ground floor was level with the sea. A grand piano had pride of place in the center of the lobby. Aurel couldn't help but go up to it. He timidly raised the keyboard lid and, standing with his arm outstretched, tinkled a few notes. A waiter came to ask him if he would like something to drink and, in passing, encouraged him to play if he felt like it.

Aurel ordered a glass of white wine and sat perched on the edge of the red upholstered piano stool. He began playing very quietly, a piece by Schumann. The waiter, setting the glass down on the piano, nodded to him encouragingly. As the woman he was waiting for was taking her time in her room, probably to make telephone calls, Aurel gradually let himself be carried away by the music. This piano was clearly a magnificent instrument. The bass notes it produced were sublime. To highlight the lower octaves, he moved on to a piece by Shostakovich. It was hardly compatible with quiet and discretion. To give the chaotic melody the fullness it deserved, Aurel began to strike the keys vigorously. Hotel employees leaned over the railings of the upper floors, which opened onto the lobby. Cooks came and stood in the kitchen door. Intrigued, a group of tourists sunbathing by the outdoor swimming pool came to see what was happening in the foyer. Aurel vaguely realized he had an audience and fell back on his old habits as a piano-bar musician. He began playing a salsa tune from the Buena Vista Social Club, responding to smiles with little cries.

Suddenly he felt a hand on his shoulder.

"Monsieur le Consul . . ."

Jocelyne Mayères. He leapt to his feet and closed the piano lid with a bang.

"Forgive me!" he said, looking around, aghast.

"I'm the one who's been taking her sweet time. I couldn't resist the pleasure of taking a shower. It's so hot here."

"Don't I know it!"

"How would you like us to proceed?"

"I have to take you to identify your brother's body. It may be a difficult moment."

"I'm a doctor, don't forget. I know about these things. But obviously, you're right, it's different for a family member."

"We have time, in any case. I suggest we go for lunch and have a bit of a talk."

"With pleasure. I'll let you choose the spot. As you know, I'm totally ignorant where this city is concerned."

They got back into the Clio and went to a Lebanese restaurant on the old coast road. For Aurel, the venue had to satisfy two conditions: have a discreet table available, and not be frequented by anyone from the embassy.

This establishment suited his requirements perfectly. A very small terrace overlooked the sea. There were only two tables, both of them free. They sat down opposite each other and ordered quickly. Right away, Jocelyne Mayères wanted Aurel to tell her the most minute details of the case. He did as she asked and finished with the commissaire's provisional conclusions.

"And what do you think?"

"Me? Well, I don't think the felony murder theory explains everything. Why would thieves have gone to the trouble of hoisting him to the top of the mast?"

"At the same time, they did break and enter, and there was theft, undeniably."

"I know, and that's where the trouble comes in."

"And the girl?"

"She wasn't raped. She lied to the police just as she was lying to your brother. She said she was living with him, but she also had an African boyfriend."

"And this boyfriend—have the police questioned him?"

"I'm not sure the police know he exists . . ."

Aurel confessed this with a mischievous smile. Adopting a modest air, he began stirring a little bowl of hummus with a piece of bread. There was a long silence, during which Jocelyne Mayères didn't take her eyes off him. Then she began laughing.

"Tell me, Monsieur le Consul, am I mistaken, or are you conducting your own investigation on the side?"

Aurel stuffed the bread into his mouth, chewed for a long while, wiped his mouth, and put his hands together, elbows on the table.

"'Investigation' is a rather grand word. Let's just say I do my own thinking and try to find out useful things. It's true I'm interested in your brother's case."

Jocelyne Mayères knew nothing about the customs of the country. She had no idea how a murder investigation was supposed to be conducted. But she trusted this strange little man. She was convinced he was telling the truth. He took an avid interest in the case, and this made him likable. He was seeking the truth. Whether it was out of simple curiosity or for other reasons didn't really matter.

"I would like you to tell me a little more about your brother."

Aurel had to stop himself from calling him Jacques.

"What can I say? I loved him very much. As children, we were very close, almost twins . . ."

The calm atmosphere, this seascape with its evocation of eternity, the gentle whisper of the waves, all suddenly caused Jocelyne Mayères to relax, after the tension of the trip and the turmoil of the arrival. She began crying softly, unable to say anything more.

Aurel let her unburden herself for a moment and looked off into the distance. He had an urge to reach for his cigarette holder but restrained himself. And he was astonished by his own behavior when he held out his hand and touched the weeping woman's fingers.

"I understand," he murmured.

"Forgive me."

She regained her composure, looked around for a tissue, and finally settled for the red paper napkin on her plate.

"When you called me, you know . . . I had been expecting that call for months . . ."

"Why? Was he threatened?"

"No. But I was afraid for him. The life he chose, to go off like that, giving everything up, I knew it was risky. It's hard to explain. Like a premonition. And besides, I knew him so well."

"You're nearly the same age . . ."

"We were only two years apart. We were the little ones. We had our big brother."

"Who died young, according to the records."

"And do you know why?"

Aurel shook his head. The waiter came by for a moment to see if everything was all right and to fill their glasses.

"Because he was a hero. Imagine that."

She said this with a touch of bitterness, as if such a quality had been the cause of the much misfortune.

"A hero in the Algerian war."

She waved her hand evasively.

"But that was so long ago. It doesn't matter. What do you want to know about Jacques?"

"You were brought up together in Haute-Savoie?"

"In a little village in the Arve Valley, across from Megève. It's called Oex. There's not much there, just a train station and a sawmill. Which was my father's. He was born in a village nearby, and his own father was a carpenter."

"Is that why Jacques developed his taste for working with wood?"

"He didn't develop a taste for working with wood. Not at all."

"So . . . his career, then . . . Do you mind if I take a few notes?"

Aurel had taken out his fake leather notebook and opened it to a blank page.

"It's fairly complicated, the life of traditional families. When you're not from the region, you can't imagine what it's like. In fact, from one valley to the next, there are rivalries. A lot of unfinished business, still haunting people's minds. Add to that the fact that this was just after the war . . ."

Aurel recalled his own childhood, the long afternoons spent with his maternal aunt, who described in detail how all their neighbors behaved during the war: "That one there, the Party section leader, don't ever forget he denounced your cousin Shlomo. Mrs. Thingummy, on the other hand, hid two families until the liberation."

"Are you interested in the stories about our valleys?"

Jocelyne Mayères had interrupted his daydreaming.

"Very much so, excuse me."

"In our region," she continued, "there were two types of men. In my mother's family, people would have said they were all heroes. Her own brother joined the Resistance during the war and was shot. But before him, there were the *carbonari*, the guys who fought alongside the French army in 1914, and there was even, so they say, a soldier of the old guard from the Grande Armée."

"What did they do when there was no war on?"

"They were crystal merchants, they hunted chamois, they were smugglers, too. All summer they roamed the mountains. In the winter, they did woodworking, but it was only while waiting for the summer season. They weren't trying to make their fortune. What they all wanted, in my mother's family, was freedom or glory."

"And on your father's side?"

"They were another sort of men: hard-working, poorly paid, sedentary. My grandfather did go up to Paris, but only to transport pianos. And the minute he had three coins to rub together, he came back to Sallanches, where he bought a café on the quai de Mont-Blanc. Then, with his son, my father, they opened a sawmill next to a little torrent in the region that we call the Rippaz."

"And what did they do during the war?"

"Well, that's just it, nothing glorious. When the Italians occupied the region, they were careful not to fight them. They got someone else to run the café. Behind it, there was a big empty building that belonged to them; the Italians turned it into barracks. Everyone suspected my father of having rented it to them, which probably wasn't true, but it shows they wouldn't have put it past him."

The sun had moved around. They were in the shade now, and the sea breeze brought some cool air. Jocelyne rolled down the sleeves of her light cardigan.

"All of which is to say that the boys in the family had two different models. Of course they were drawn more to their mother's side. When we were little, Jacques always played resistance fighter. He loved wandering around the mountain. He caught birds, God knows how. With bits of wire, he made a cage that he filled with robins and titmice. I'm sure he would have wanted to lead a different life."

"What stopped him?"

"The death of our older brother. He admired him tremendously. He was his god. He was tall, and handsome, and very brave. When he was eighteen, he enlisted, and they sent him to Algeria. Jacques was crazy with enthusiasm and impatience. If he'd been old enough, he would have done exactly the same thing. Our mother said nothing. But she had this silent way of encouraging him . . ."

"When exactly did your older brother die?"

"In 1961, just before the end of the war. Jacques was eleven, and I was thirteen. He had a big map in his bedroom, and in the evening, depending on the news, he would pin a little flag on the map so he could follow the position of Corporal Mayères. One day it was a cross that Jacques pinned on the map."

Nervously, she raised her glass to her lips, but it was empty. Aurel hurried to refill it.

"For me it was a tragedy. The death of a brother I loved. But for Jacques, the shock was twofold. It meant not only would he never see his older brother again, but also that he would have to replace him. Because my father needed someone to take over the business."

"So Jacques took over from your father even though it wasn't what he wanted?"

"He wanted anything but. But where we come from, you don't question your parents' opinion. Even my mother was powerless to save him from that fate."

Aurel was thinking, nibbling on his pencil.

"What happened, then, that he put so much energy into it and was such a success?"

"In the beginning, I can assure you he dragged his feet. He worked as little as possible and then went off hunting birds again. It could have gone on like that for a long time. But then he met her."

"His wife?"

"Yes, his future wife."

"How did they meet?"

"Her parents were clients. She came along with her father one day. Jacques saw her and fell madly in love."

"Had he . . . how to put it . . . had other experiences, before?"

"I don't think so. He was fairly shy and antisocial. The stationmaster, who lived next door, had tried to get him to marry one of his daughters. He had four. But we had known them all our lives, and Jacques thought of them as playmates, rather. And anyway they were all kind of mannish and not very attractive."

"Whereas Aimée—"

"Aimée was an elf. She lived in town. She had fine white hands and light eyes."

"You didn't like her."

"I did my utmost to try to keep Jacques from marrying her. She knows it, and she's always held it against me."

"What didn't you like about her?"

"I think I was a little jealous, of course, like a sister whose brother is about to be stolen from her. But it wasn't just that. I felt she was dangerous."

"Was she the one who seduced him?"

"Not at all. I have to give her credit for that. In the beginning, she had nothing but scorn for Jacques. She was aiming higher."

"Was her family rich? I saw on the internet that the Delachats were wealthy entrepreneurs."

"Except she wasn't from that branch of the family. Her father ran a little tobacconist's. They lived very meanly, and the fortune of the 'other Delachats' was an ongoing source of jealousy and suffering. Her mother was constantly talking about the dresses and hats of a certain Madame Delachat whom she, unfortunately, did not happen to be—about her exotic travels, her apartments in Paris and in Cannes, her cars. Whereas she, on the other hand, had to copy the patterns in fashion magazines to have the latest Paris styles made up on the cheap. She dreamt of a fine match for her daughter, to get her out of there."

"But your father was head of a company, after all. And Jacques was set to take over . . ."

"A little Alpine sawmill: do you think that could satisfy old mother Delachat's ambitions?"

"Did Jacques realize?"

"He was in love. He was prepared to move heaven and earth. It was as if this was his combat: the more inaccessible Aimée became, the harder he fought to get her."

"He'd found a trace of the family heroism . . ."

"Perhaps. The fact remains that he went courting all on his own. He would go to see Aimée in Bonneville. He gave her presents. He spent all his money on her. Nothing put him off."

"And so he prevailed?"

"I think if they'd found a better option, the Delachats wouldn't have given in. But in the end the mother figured that, for want of a good catch, her daughter had better take a man who was well brought up, promising, and malleable, and put him to work: she would guide him step-by-step, make him climb the rungs to fortune and success. And he would do it all for *her*."

"So Aimée helped him get ahead in his career?"

"Not on your life! Her mother had warned her: above all, don't go getting your hands dirty, don't ever go playing check-out clerk or accountant, let alone cook or cleaning lady. In a word, don't lift a finger, stick only to getting presents and admiration. Be a queen, a muse. And turn income into luxury, luxury into need, need into demand, so that the husband will work harder than ever."

"And it worked."

"Beyond all their expectations, probably. Jacques bent over backwards for his wife. He began working like a crazy man and never stopped. Nothing was good enough for her. She wanted money, servants, houses: he gave them to her. And if she didn't ask for anything, he offered . . ."

Aurel closed his eyes. It felt good when reality confirmed daydreams and intuition in this way. He felt a shiver of ease, like a chess player who sees the strategy he's been perfecting over the last several moves suddenly pay off. He hadn't foreseen everything, to be sure, but he was right about the basics. Aurel thought about his aunt: she had said he had something of a medium about him, and she used to tease him, calling him a little wizard.

"What's the matter? Do you feel unwell?"

Aurel came to himself, flustered.

"Oh, it's nothing, nothing, forgive me. The Tropics, you know . . . Would you believe, I have relapses of malaria . . ."

V

They had to hurry, to get to the morgue before closing time. The identification of the body, as expected, was a difficult moment. Jocelyne Mayères said she would like to be on her own for a while afterwards. Aurel had the driver take her back to the Radisson.

He used the time to go by the office before nightfall. The car dropped him off at the corner of the coast road, and he went the rest of the way on foot. It was a good way to work through his emotions. He had used the pretext of Mayères's sister's visit to have a look at the body, as well. In comparison with the photograph he had on his computer, the true face of the deceased man was hardly recognizable. For a start, he had aged, which was normal, because the photograph was an old one. And then, by relaxing his features, death had eliminated any remnants of tension, hardness, or ambition from his face. It would have been an exaggeration to say that only serenity remained, but there was a little of that all the same. The word relief was what came to mind.

Because of his background, Aurel believed that the dead were present among us. In the Romanian countryside where he was born, the dead were there: attentive, protective, or evil. Most peasant rituals sought to neutralize them, to tame them, or to ward them off. In his family, on his mother's side, they had nothing but scorn for these magical practices. But on his father's side, where they were both Vlachs and Magyars, they did not joke about such matters. And so, Aurel was convinced that while it was he who had been gazing at Mayères in the photograph over recent days, today it was the dead man who had looked at him. He had given him a pale smile, frozen in death, during those few short moments when the attendant had lifted the blue sheet covering the body.

The coolness of the evening air was only relative, because in the darkness the ground and the stones gave off all the heat stocked up during the day. And yet, in spite of his tweed suit and his trench coat buttoned top to bottom, Aurel shivered on opening the door to his office.

He found Hassan waiting for him, crouching on the floor by the far wall. The young Guinean man leapt to his feet. Aurel had almost forgotten he had sent him on a mission.

"Where were you?"

Aurel hated the way the white inhabitants often used the familiar *tu* with Africans, while the Africans went on saying *vous*. But with Hassan, Aurel used *tu* for another reason altogether. Aurel was twenty-five years older than Hassan, and the age gap gave him permission to look on him as a son.

"At Lamine's."

"Ah, that's right. Well?"

"Well, the police got there before me."

"They seem to be well-informed."

"I'm not sure they knew about Mame Fatim and him. I saw his cousin. He told me they were looking for Lamine because he's a petty criminal. He's been convicted of theft several times. And he also works as an informant now and again."

"Did they pick him up?"

"No. He'd already vanished by the time they got there."

"This cousin, is he a petty criminal, too?"

"Not at all. Besides, they don't live in the same house. The cousin is much older. He's a very pious man who works at city hall, for the water department."

"Do you know him well?"

"He's related to my mother. They come from the same village, at the foot of the Fouta Djallon."

"Did he tell you anything interesting?"

"Not at first. You know what it's like in our culture. You have to sit down, drink some tea, take your time. The police were in too much of a hurry. He didn't tell them anything."

"Whereas you . . ."

Hassan smiled. Aurel was a man who understood things. That was why he liked him.

Aurel sat down in his armchair and turned on the computer. He was glad to see Mayères's usual face. It banished the other one, the one he'd seen in the morgue.

"So tell me. What did he say to you?"

"For a start," Hassan said slowly, unconsciously imitating the cousin's confidential tone, "this Lamine disappeared the night of the murder. His door is locked, but there's a balcony in front of his bedroom window. The cousin sent his grandson there yesterday to see if he could get in that way."

"Why would the cousin want to do that?"

"Because the little apartment where Lamine has been living belongs to him. And he owes him several months' rent."

"Ah, now I see. And so, the kid?"

"He got in. He found the place empty. No more clothes in the wardrobe, no more Nike, no more baseball caps. Apparently Lamine goes around trying to look sort of American. Like a rapper."

"I see," said Aurel with a sigh.

He had often tried to imagine what hell must be like. He had come to the conclusion that it was a place not unlike Conakry, particularly where the temperature was concerned, and in addition, rap music would be constantly blaring from huge loudspeakers.

"Do you have any idea where he might've gone?"

"He'd have plenty of options. He's a small-time dealer. He

has contacts in the underworld all over Guinea but also in Bissau, Gambia, and above all Sierra Leone."

"Did the police get into his place?"

"They knocked on the door and went away again. The cousin got the impression he was just a name on a long list."

"Okay, Hassan, thank you."

Aurel was dying to pour himself a glass of Tokaji, and he didn't want to do it in front of Hassan, who was Muslim. But his assistant hadn't finished. He leaned forward and spoke more quietly.

"There's something else, Monsieur le Consul."

"What is it?"

Hassan looked from left to right as if someone might be listening.

"The cousin talked about the girl, Mame Fatim."

"He knows her?"

"Yes, she used to spend the night with Lamine often."

"Even after she started living with Mayères?"

"Apparently that didn't change anything. The cousin even wondered whether Lamine wasn't being kept by her. And by two other girls he brought home from time to time."

Prudish Hassan's morality was visibly shocked by such behavior. He only shared these details with his eyes lowered, and must have been inwardly murmuring words of submission to God and the Prophet.

"Well, that's not very surprising, after all. Most of these young girls must have pimps. Is that everything?"

"No," continued Hassan, his eyes shining, "that's not the interesting part in what the cousin said."

"So what is it?"

"He told me . . . that she was there, in Lamine's room, the night the *toubab* was murdered."

"What?"

Aurel suddenly forgot about his white wine. Leaning over the desk, he spoke to the young Guinean eyeball to eyeball.

"What are you talking about? She wasn't on the boat? Then why did they find her there that morning?"

Hassan sat up straight and looked offended.

"I'm just telling you what the cousin told me, in secret."

"What did he say *exactly*?"

"That night, he couldn't sleep. From time to time, he gets migraines, and they give him bad dreams that wake him up. In their little street, you can hear everything. Next door there was a baby teething, and it was crying."

"So what!"

"At around midnight, the cousin heard a car. To get there, taxis have to go slow because the road is full of potholes. He heard it coming from some ways off. And then it stopped outside his house. Since he wasn't asleep, he went over to the window. That's when he saw Lamine and Mame Fatim get out of the taxi and go into the house across the street."

"He's sure it was her? If the guy has other girlfriends . . ."

"Sure as can be. The other ones don't have the same hairstyle. And what's more, she got out of the car first, and turned around to face the cousin's windows while she waited for Lamine to pay the driver. There was no doubt. It was her."

"At midnight, you said?"

"Roughly."

"And they stayed all night?"

"That, the cousin doesn't know."

"He didn't hear them leave?"

"No, because he took tranquilizers in the middle of the night, and that knocked him out. He woke up late the following morning."

Aurel was thinking fast. He looked at Mayères's portrait. He seemed to perceive something painful in his eyes, something resigned, which he had not noticed before. But what did it mean?

"Thank you, Hassan. This is precious information you've

obtained. I absolutely have to get to the bottom of it. Was she on the boat with Mayères earlier that evening? If she was, why did she leave, and how? And above all, I'd like to understand how she got back there the following morning."

Hassan reflected, but he had no idea, either.

"Listen, I'd like to ask you a favor. It will require an effort, I know, and you can make up for it later on with two extra days off. But here's the thing: I need you to go to the marina tonight. See who hangs around there at the end of the day. There must be a security guard, or kids, I don't know. Go over there and dig up what you can about the night in question."

Hassan, too, was beginning to enjoy this parallel investigation. He agreed enthusiastically.

"Here's some money for the taxi and your expenses. Try and have dinner there, go for a drink in a cabana behind there on the beach. Well, you'll see."

Hassan took the money and disappeared down the passageway.

Aurel reached for the bottle of white wine he always kept in his office, chilled, thanks to a tiny fridge he had installed at his own expense. He poured himself a glass and drank it, tipping back in his chair.

It was obvious that nothing about this murder made any sense. That was why it was fascinating. Aurel didn't like straightforward events. He liked to think that things were always more complicated than they seemed. He could easily picture conspiracies behind the events in the news, and most of the time his theories were somewhat far-fetched. This time, to his great delight, he was sure he was *truly* confronted with a mystery. At last he would be able to put to good use the mental gymnastics he ordinarily practiced in a void. He looked at Mayères on the screen and raised his glass.

"We'll find those bastards who did this to you!"

Drinking made Aurel dreamy and brotherly. He was about

to reach for the bottle to pour a second round to the victim and himself when his gaze fell on the computer clock in the lower right-hand corner of the screen. It read 19:30. He had told Jocelyne Mayères he would pick her up at the hotel and take her to dinner. They would be able to continue the conversation that had been interrupted by the visit to the morgue.

He ran home. In the dark night of Conakry, you could hear people conversing at their doors, and the sounds of the television wafting through open windows. The smells of fried fat and hot pepper lingered in some of the narrower passageways. To Aurel, they evoked childhood memories of summer days when he used to go with his mother to the market. Peasants came from all over to display their meats and cheeses. Aurel's mother hurried past the stalls, saying each time that everything was repulsive. Which was probably why he still felt a vague disgust.

Once he was home, he opened all the drawers and shoved things around in the wardrobe to find something suitable to wear. He had a precise and, to be honest, fairly old-fashioned notion about the clothes a man should wear when taking a lady to dinner. This, too, he had inherited from his mother, and his marriage had not lasted long enough for his manners to change. He put on a white shirt with poorly ironed sleeves. Which didn't matter because he had no intention of removing his jacket. The double-breasted black suit he wore over it was a bit worn at the elbows. It was true he'd had it made in Leipzig nearly twenty years earlier by one of his cousins who was a tailor. He always knotted his bow ties himself, convinced that if he bought the kind that were already knotted he would look like some sort of maître d'hôtel. But it cost him a good five minutes of standing annoyed in front of the mirror. As usual, his mother-of-pearl cufflinks were nowhere to be found, and he had to wear the everyday ones of yellow gold. In the time it took to comb his hair and brush his teeth, he was outside, locking the door and hailing a taxi.

He found Jocelyne Mayères in the lobby, dressed in pink summer trousers and a lightweight white shirt. She gave the consul's get-up a curious look, but now that she'd been in his company since that morning, nothing more surprised her. In the taxi, he'd had a think and concluded that the easiest thing would be to stay at the Radisson for dinner. She must be tired, and he hadn't had time to ask anyone to recommend a suitable restaurant.

She applauded his suggestion. A few minutes later, they were sitting at a square table next to the swimming pool. The African sky cast over them its dark blue veil, studded with twinkling points of light. On the tables around them oil lamps formed halos illuminating the diners' faces.

"I can see why my brother came to love this country," said Jocelyne. "There is so much sweetness and sensuality."

Aurel gave a crooked smile.

"Yes, yes."

"You don't seem to like it here."

"It's . . . because of the heat. I don't deal with the heat very well."

"I see."

She looked at his thick suit, his buttoned shirt. She would have liked to suggest that perhaps, if he dressed differently, the heat might be more bearable. But she realized that Aurel's discomfort was not only climatic. Curiosity led her to question him about his past.

"Forgive me if I am indiscreet—"

"Not at all!"

"Wait, I haven't asked anything yet."

She laughed. He was so uncomfortable, and his embarrassment so predictable.

"You have foreign origins, I believe."

"Romanian. I was born in Romania."

"But to be a French consul—"

"You have to be French. Is that what you're wondering?"

He had figured she would ask eventually. Everyone did, sooner or later.

"You know," he said, pretending to look at the wine list, even when he knew very well what he was going to order, "under communism, there were countries that sold their citizens."

"Sold them!"

"Yes. If you had family in the West, you could obtain a visa to go and join them, in exchange for a certain amount of money."

"So you were bought?"

"Yes, and I can tell you exactly how much I am worth."

"How much?"

"Twelve thousand dollars."

"Really?"

"Does that surprise you? Oh, I can see you wouldn't have paid that much for me . . ."

"Of course I would . . . What makes you say that?"

It was a joke Aurel made every time. He gave a tired laugh.

"I'm just joking. Ignore what I said."

The waitress came to take the order for their drinks.

"What would you say to a bottle of white wine?" Then, leaning forward, he added, "White wine travels better than red."

"White is fine with me. And some mineral water, please."

The waitress went away. She must have the same sensual figure and languid walk as Mame Fatim. Both of them, looking at her, thought of Mayères and his murder.

"Poor Jacques," said Jocelyne Mayères. "What a sad life he had. I hope he at least had some good times here, before he died."

"He wasn't happy in France?"

"As I was saying, he worked like a dog. Never any vacation, never any rest."

"Any hobbies?"

"Not really. No, wait: he collected things from the Algerian war. You know, badges, bits of uniform, newspapers from the era, that sort of thing."

"In memory of your brother?"

"I'm sure. As I told you, he never got over not being a hero, too, never got over having taken after his father—business, a quiet life, was how he put it. But over time, his hobby became a skill, as well, like everything he did. Apparently he was an authority in the field. Collectors from all over the world wrote to him."

"What became of the collection?"

"He donated it to the Musée de l'Armée before he left. There was a little ceremony in the halls of the Invalides. A thank you from the military."

"All the same, that must have pleased him?"

"It was strange. I was there with my husband. We got the feeling that Jacques was even sadder with all those high-ranking officers around him. He gave a speech devoted entirely to our brother. And he was on the verge of tears."

Aurel had taken out his notebook and was jotting down notes, his handwriting completely distorted because the little lamp on the table hardly gave any light.

"Were there any weapons in his collection?"

"I think there were quite a few. Assault rifles from the era, daggers reserved for the special forces, hand grenades, that sort of thing."

"And he gave them to the museum, too?"

"I think so."

"All of them?"

"That I don't know."

This had not yet occurred to Aurel: why hadn't Mayères fought back? The commissaire would have told him if he'd found any weapons on board.

"You started telling me about his wife, this morning."

"What else would you like to know?"

"You still despise her, don't you?"

"I can't judge her. She is who she is. All that mattered to me is that she took Jacques away from his family. From me in particular. She wanted him all to herself."

"Did they separate a long time ago?"

"It happened gradually. He bought an apartment on the Côte d'Azur, and she began spending more and more time there. They also had a pied-à-terre in Paris, near Saint-Augustin. She never liked Haute-Savoie. She eventually stopped going there altogether. Jacques had to go where she was. And so, inevitably, with all the work he had, they saw less of each other."

"Did she have lovers?"

"He never mentioned any. But it wouldn't surprise me. In any event, she would have been discreet about it. She certainly wouldn't want to run the risk of a divorce where she was at fault. She cares too much about money."

From time to time, the strains of an orchestra reached them, coming no doubt from a bar on the beach a bit further along the coast road.

"She's in for a rude awakening."

"Why do you say that?"

"You know that your brother, after he sold his company to the Chinese, closed all his accounts."

"Yes, and?"

"And it looks as if he took everything with him."

"Took everything with him . . . on the boat?"

"Yes. And as you know, his safe was robbed."

"But that's madness, to have so much money on board a sailboat!"

"Madness, perhaps. But it was above all a way of depriving his wife. Because they had a joint property agreement. Half of it was hers. By taking it all with him, he was ruining her. And by dying, he disinherited her."

"Do you think she knows?"

"I don't know. I'm going to call her tomorrow morning. It will be a chance to see how she reacts."

Jocelyne was still reeling from the revelation.

"Whatever the case may be," stammered Aurel, "when you see the French commissaire who's in charge of the investigation, don't mention any of this. He's a fairly . . . traditional man. He would know you got it from me, and he would think I'm being eccentric."

Jocelyne Mayères looked at Aurel, with his crooked bow tie, his starched shirt, and the pin representing the Romanian eagle on the lapel of his worn suit. She hid a smile in her glass of white wine. She would hate to contribute to the notion that Aurel Timescu might be eccentric . . .

* * *

Aurel slept badly that night. For a long time he wondered if he'd drunk too much or not enough. Finally, at three in the morning, he opened a new bottle.

He couldn't unravel what disturbed him the most: the things he had found out during the day and the increasingly complex insight into Mayères's death they offered, or the message from Baudry he'd found on his answering machine when he got home. The consul general had been told by Lemenêtrier that Aurel had helped himself to a file regarding a murder. Now he was congratulating him on it, his manner clearly hypocritical. But he also advised him—and his tone of voice implied *ordered*—to stick to the strictly consular aspects of the case.

Stupid idiot, thought Aurel, his intuition is always spot-on when it comes to humiliating me.

Baudry added that he would be back in Conakry by the middle of next week (in other words, two days earlier than Aurel had expected him) and that he would send for him as soon as he arrived for a detailed report on his activities.

And so Aurel had only five days left to conduct his investigation. If he didn't come up with anything, he would no longer have access to the file. The prospect upset him greatly. To be sure, his enthusiasm for the affair contained a significant element of curiosity and pride, because he didn't want to fail. But now there was also this strange complicity he had with Mayères. He felt as if he knew him and, strangely, as if he owed him something. As if fate had chosen him, Aurel, to obtain justice for this man who had been so cravenly murdered.

A knocking at his door at eight o'clock roused him from his bed. It was Hassan, there to report on his mission at the marina. Aurel had advised him, the day before, to come to his house, as it would be more discreet. In the morning, there were always people hanging around in the corridors of the consulate, and you could never be sure you wouldn't be overheard. Aurel slipped on a dressing gown, monogrammed with his initials, and went to open the door. Then he asked Hassan to wait for him for a moment while he took a quick shower to wake up.

All through his childhood, Aurel had dreamt of hot water; in Africa, it was cold water he missed. The water tank on the roof started to heat up as soon as the sun rose. And it was impossible, except in the middle of the night, to get anything other than steaming hot water from the tap. After his shower, he rubbed himself with some vetiver he had bought in Paris two years earlier, which he used only for special occasions (he had put some on before his dinner with Jocelyne Mayères).

He led Hassan into the kitchen. As he stubbornly refused

to resort to the services of a cleaning lady—a profession with which he was at war on the grounds of broken objects and disturbed papers—the kitchen was an indescribably dirty mess. Aurel could manage regardless. He found two tea bags among the clutter piled on the counter, filled a kettle, and washed two cups with cracked rims. Then, in lieu of breakfast, he lit a cold cigarette butt.

"So, last night? Good catch?"

It was clear that Hassan had not slept much either. He had trouble keeping his eyes open as he watched Aurel preparing the tea.

"Uh . . . yes!"

"Did you find out anything interesting?"

"There's a guy there called Seydou. He's sort of the caretaker. He lives in a hut in front of the clubhouse."

"I've met him, but I didn't see his hut."

"It's sort of hidden in the trees. But from where he is, he has a good view of the marina, and he can hear everything."

"Was he at home on the night of the crime?"

"Of course. He never leaves his post."

"And did he see any movement that night?"

"He was a bit reluctant to talk about it. Because the police asked him the same thing, and he didn't tell them anything. We talked for a long time. I told him he'd have more to fear if he kept silent."

"What is he afraid of?"

"Well, here's the thing: when Mame Fatim started living with Mayères, she came to a little agreement with Seydou. Almost every evening, he went to get her, and she spent part of the night on land."

"With Lamine?"

"Yes. And the thing is that Seydou is afraid that Ravigot, the marina manager, will fire him if he finds out he's been involved in any little money-making schemes. Specially as apparently the other boats also pay him to perform similar favors."

"You think his boss doesn't know? He sleeps there, too . . ."

"Yes, but since most nights he's drunk, he has no idea what goes on."

"So, what exactly did he tell you about the night in question?"

"That night, Mame Fatim asked him to come and fetch her with his skiff at ten o'clock. Lamine was waiting for her in a taxi by the entrance to the marina."

"And Mayères?"

"He was asleep."

"Dead drunk, too?"

"No, according to Seydou, Mame Fatim put a sleeping tablet in his drink in the evening."

"Every evening?"

"Probably just when she wanted to go out. I didn't ask."

"So, she went off in the taxi with Lamine. They went to his place. When did she come back?"

"That's where Seydou's not very precise."

"He's not precise, or he's lying?"

"No, I don't think he's hiding anything. His explanation was perfectly clear."

Aurel had gone into the bathroom and was getting dressed while Hassan spoke to him from the living room. But when he got to this point in the story, Aurel came out so as not to miss any of his reply.

"Go on."

"Seydou had had a rough day. One of the boats had left the day before. He'd had to run around on errands with the crew members. He'd had to row out all the supplies which some newcomers had ordered in town. He was exhausted. After he dropped Mame Fatim off, he went to bed. He didn't hear her come back. It was only in the morning, when he saw the body at the top of the mast, that he also noticed that someone had used his skiff during the night. The oar hadn't been put back the way he usually leaves it."

"So we don't know when Mame Fatim got back?"

"No."

"Lamine might have rowed her back himself using Seydou's boat?"

"That's what he thinks."

Aurel reflected for a long while. This information strengthened Dupertuis's theory. Mayères must have been asleep when Mame Fatim and her boyfriend came back to the sailboat. Everything seemed to point to them. And yet, Aurel still felt a nagging, inexplicable doubt.

"What else did you find out?" he finally asked Hassan, whose eyes were heavy with fatigue.

"From Seydou, nothing. But afterwards, I took a walk around. There are some guys with pirogues who sleep on the beach. They never go into the marina, but they can see what's going on."

"And?"

"So apparently it's a hub for coke."

"Coke? As in cocaine?"

"Yes. It comes here from Colombia by way of the Bissagos Islands and Guinea-Bissau."

"Everybody knows that."

"And then, from here, there are several possible onward routes. By air—"

"I know all this. People are constantly telling us about mules boarding flights for Europe. There are also overland smugglers, who cross the Sahara on foot or by truck."

"Yes, and there are yachts."

"I thought they usually stashed their merchandise on cargo ships."

"Sailboats, too. The marina here is reputed to be a stopover."

Aurel, while listening to Hassan, was shaving methodically. In truth, nature had only blessed him with three hairy spots: on either side of his chin, and a little mustache beneath his nose. The rest was hopelessly smooth. And yet, he smeared the shaving cream almost up to his forehead, and ran his razor delicately over his entire face.

"You think Mayères would have been dabbling in any of that? He had a safe full of money!"

"I don't know," said Hassan, a bit vexed. "I'm passing on the information, is all."

"Has there ever been any trouble here? Gangland killings . . ."

"No. It's quiet. But local people say there's bound to be stuff going on."

Aurel came out of the bathroom, buttoning his shirt.

"Right, thank you very much. You've done a good job."

On saying this, he went and took a metal box from a side table, opened it, and offered Hassan a slice of sweet bread. It was a pastry his paternal grandmother used to make at Christmas.

"Here," he said, "have some cozonac. I made it myself."

Hassan looked at the bread, somewhat astonished. But nothing surprised him anymore, coming from Aurel.

"Okay, son, you can go home now and go to bed."

It was nine a.m, the time he'd planned to call Aimée Mayères in France. With everything he now knew about the deceased man's wife, he was more fearful than ever about her reaction. Though he wouldn't admit it to himself, by letting some time go by before calling her, he had vaguely hoped that someone else might have informed her and that he wouldn't have to experience her initial shock. Whatever the case might be, he could no longer prevaricate.

He dialed the number the lawyer had given him. The area code was for the Var *département*. There was an answer on the second ring.

"I would like to speak to Madame Mayères, please."

A woman on the other end replied in a North African accent.

"She's just getting up. She's having her coffee."

Aurel checked his watch. It was noon in France.

"It's urgent."

"I'll go see. May I please ask who's calling?"

"The consul of France in Guinea."

He could hear some whispering, the sound of a cup, then footsteps. The lady was taking her time.

"Yes?"

"Madame Aimée Mayères?"

"Speaking."

Her voice was rather forced, the intonation snobbish, haughty.

Aurel introduced himself and indulged in long, dilatory preamble before getting to the point.

"I am calling to inform you that your husband, Monsieur Jacques Mayères, has died."

"Ah," said the woman simply.

It was neither cry nor sob, just an acknowledgment.

Since this first bite had been swallowed without difficulty, Aurel decided to proceed with the next one.

"He was murdered on his sailboat."

"Right."

Still no obvious emotion.

"Perhaps you already knew?"

"No. This is the first I've heard."

Aurel was somewhat disconcerted.

"Do you . . . do you think you will come to Conakry?"

"My health will not allow it."

From her tone, it was obvious that her health had nothing to do with it. She simply couldn't be bothered and wasn't hiding the fact. She was clearly the sort of woman with whom it was pointless to appeal to feelings. Aurel returned to more concrete, practical topics.

"What arrangements do you envisage for the funeral?"

"What is usual in these cases?"

"These cases, Madame, are not very common. It all depends on the family's wishes. If they would like to repatriate the body—"

"Look, Monsieur le Consul, my husband left France without any intention of returning. Unless his lawyer is aware of some other arrangement—"

"I spoke to him. He didn't mention any."

"In that case, let us respect his wishes. Let him be buried where he died."

"As you like. Something else: in terms of the succession, you ought to know that Monsieur Mayères's safe, the one he had installed on his sailboat, was completely emptied by his aggressors. There is nothing left."

"So?"

Her voice did not sound any more upset than when he had told her about the murder. Her indifference surprised him. It went counter to the image he had of Aimée Mayères. While he understood she might show no emotion on hearing that her husband had died, he had expected more of a reaction to the news that his fortune had disappeared.

"So? But this money was meant to be yours, I imagine."

"Look, Monsieur le Consul, my husband and I have not been in touch for several years. We settled our affairs. I received what I felt he owed me. The rest doesn't belong to me. I might even add: it doesn't interest me. I have what I need to live on and don't need anything else. Is that clear?"

"Absolutely clear, Madame."

"Is there anything else?"

"Well, I would like to know if you intend to take action."

"Do you mean press charges?"

"Yes. When a French citizen dies a violent death in a foreign country, the court starts a preliminary investigation. I won't hide from you the fact that it generally doesn't get very far."

"And if the family presses charges?"

"Then the proceedings might be undertaken more robustly. A rogatory commission might be sent. The judge can ask to see witnesses . . . It all takes time, of course, and we cannot be sure of getting at the truth."

Silence at the other end of the line. Aurel couldn't hear anything, not even breathing.

"The truth," Aimée Mayères echoed at last, her voice icy. "In an affair like this, Monsieur le Consul, the truth can only be sordid, and I do not wish to hear it. I have enough happy memories of my husband not to seek to ruin them with indiscreet details about his death."

"So you won't be pressing charges?"

"No. Is there anything else I can help you with?"

"I don't think so."

"In that case, thank you for your trouble. Goodbye, Monsieur le Consul. Maître Hochard will take care of all the details."

"Thank you, Madame. Goodbye."

Aurel sat for a long while staring at the telephone he had just put down. Mayères's face, on the computer screen, seemed more foreign to him than ever. He thought he had understood him, had come up with his theories, and now he saw them all collapse. The woman he had just spoken to didn't fit the story he'd told himself during the night. She was in no way the ambitious woman eager for money, a femme fatale who must have subjected her husband to an overweening desire for social advancement. The woman he had just spoken to was a true Roman, a cold, dignified woman, pleased with her lot. After all, it was possible to combine the two images and suppose that she had become this way late in life, once her ambition had been satisfied and her passion had declined. And yet, something didn't seem right. Either the image he'd formed of the couple was wrong, or, if it was right, this woman had been putting on an act. But to what purpose?

A little while later, Aurel left the house and jogged over to the embassy.

As he was crossing the main courtyard to reach the consular building, an old man wearing a light blue suit called out to him from a distance. It was Marcelly, a retired French attorney whose family had been established in Conakry for generations, and who had stayed on in the country during the dark years. He was a member of every possible club, from the Commanderie des Vins de Bordeaux to the Compagnons Rôtisseurs, by way of the Chevaliers de l'Armagnac. Aurel was fond of him, because he had horse-and-buggy manners and was always extremely well turned out.

"You're the very person I came to see," said Marcelly, shaking Aurel's hand warmly. "I've just come from the visa section, and Lemenêtrier told me that, at the moment, you are representing the consulate in all official matters."

If Lemenêtrier had said that, it surely meant that Marcelly's proposition would involve some chore of little interest. If it meant representing the consulate at a Rotary Club meeting, Lemenêtrier wouldn't have passed the baton so eagerly.

"What can I help you with, Maître?"

"Well, of course you know that I'm president of the Association of Members of the National Order of Merit in Conakry."

Overseas, and particularly in Africa, French honors and awards were particularly sought after. Some people did not hesitate to besiege diplomatic authorities for years in order to obtain them. For their members, associations of the kind that

Marcelly presided over perpetuated the memory of the efforts they'd put in to deserve their awards.

"It just so happens that this evening," the old lawyer continued, "we are organizing a little ceremony in honor of poor Mayères, so cruelly killed on his sailboat."

Aurel gave a start.

"I thought your members were all residents."

"Indeed they are. But if members who are just passing through want to join us for the duration of their stay, they are very welcome. Wherever we go, we are ex officio members of all the local associations."

"That is a great privilege," said Aurel, feigning admiration he was far from feeling.

He had always loathed gatherings of this nature. Wherever he went, there was only one right he demanded: to be left alone.

"The consulate is duty bound to be present at this tribute. I am sure that if Monsieur le Consul Général were here—"

"At what time is your meeting, and where?"

"At seven o'clock, at l'Ancien Cercle."

"You can count on me, Maître."

As he went up to his office, Aurel thought that this would be a good opportunity to meet the people who had known Mayères. But what had he been doing in this association of doddering old men? Did they go and seek him out, or did he attend of his own free will? Aurel needed to get to the bottom of it.

When he arrived at his door, he found it locked and had a moment of anxiety. Had Baudry confiscated everything he'd so recently obtained? But then he remembered that Hassan had gone home to go to bed. No one else had the key. He opened the door. The first thing he did was pick up the telephone and call the gendarmes to tell them that Madame Jocelyne Mayères would be coming to see him just before noon. He asked them to inform him when she arrived so he could come down to greet her and go with her to see Dupertuis.

He had almost two hours ahead of him. He took the time to sit at his computer and further research this Aimée person, whom he found very intriguing. He'd had a thought about her during the night and wanted to look into it.

Aimée Mayères was easy to find on the internet: she loved all sorts of clubs and collected honorary positions in the most varied organizations. The things she seemed to like most were charitable circles. Not the kind that require activism on the ground; she had no liking for hospitals, food banks, shelters. What she liked was high-society philanthropy: fundraising dinners where they spoke about the poor while showing off their most expensive couture. Aurel found a considerable number of articles from local newspapers and the websites of towns or associations where Aimée Mayères was featured, dressed like a Christmas tree, holding facsimile cardboard checks, receiving bouquets of flowers, speaking on stage to a black-tie audience. This much he had expected. But there was something else he was looking for. An article in the *Var-Matin* gave him a lead. It showed Aimée on a dock signaling the departure for a regatta. Following this lead, Aurel soon saw his hunch confirmed: the sailboat—that had been Mayères's wife. Aurel's reasoning was simple: Jacques Mayères, the mountain man, passionate about hunting chamois and Alpine birds, had no reason to end up on a sailboat. Whereas Aimée, who now lived on the shores of the Mediterranean, seemed to have always had an interest in the sea.

In another article published in *Le Dauphiné* ten years earlier, Mayères and his wife discussed their passion for sailing. They had met with the journalist on board their sailboat moored in the harbor at La Rochelle. Mayères was getting ready to cross the Atlantic with a skipper. In answer to the journalist's questions, he said: "It's my wife who introduced to me to the sea. They have a long tradition of yachting in her family."

Digging deeper, Aurel found out that the Delachats had indeed been the owners of a yacht in the Mediterranean in the 1950s. That must have been the prosperous side of the family. They must have boasted about having become yachts-men, and this was yet another source of envy for the impov-erished side.

Which meant the story might go like this: given her deter-mination to imitate her glorious, despicable cousins, Aimée had decided very early on that ownership of a yacht was a vital emblem of success. She had pushed Mayères in that direction. After—apparently—he began to share this passion, each of them had cultivated it in his or her manner: Mayères by con-tinuing to sail or by dreaming of it, and eventually setting off on his own boat after selling his business; Aimée by living by the sea and participating assiduously in all the chic nautical events along the Côte d'Azur. Several articles showed her looking tipsy, to various degrees, at social gatherings on lux-ury sailboats or in the ports of the Mediterranean. She was personally a contributing member of the Cannes Yacht Club. These documents shed light on parts of the story, but there was still one important thing to check. Among all the people Aimée was seen with in the photographs—and she seemed quite well-acquainted with a few of them—were there any who might actually be in Guinea? Among the faces of those partygoers, could there be the missing link connecting Aimée to Conakry? As soon as Hassan came back in, he would have him follow up this lead. He absolutely had to find out who had been through the marina over these last few weeks. Assuming he managed to do this, it would then imply a huge labor of cross-checking to see whether the itinerary of any of the boats pointed to a connection with Madame Mayères. The probability was obviously quite low, but in an investigation, you had to factor in luck. Aurel didn't have time to go further into that aspect because the guard on duty called to inform him that Jocelyne Mayères had arrived. Aurel turned off his computer and went down at a run.

VI

When he was a young man in Romania dreaming of France, Aurel had formed a certain image of French elegance. The elegance of the women, of course, but also the men. His notions went no further than what he had gleaned from novels by Maupassant, ideas that were brought up to date by films from the 1930s. He realized that walking sticks, hats, and tie pins had disappeared. But he still believed that well-tailored suits and fine fabric mattered to the French. What he discovered when he finally made it to France filled him with dismay. He never quite got used to the crumpled trousers, ill-assorted colors, yellow shoes worn with blue suits and other heresies he encountered on a daily basis. The moment he entered the office of commissaire Dupertuis with Jocelyne Mayères, Aurel came upon the usual dispiriting spectacle. God alone knew where the policeman could have unearthed a jacket like that, such a horrible check that it hurt your eyes to look at it. His assistant, summoned for the occasion, was wearing red trousers (red!), and a third man, probably a military aid worker, was in jeans and white shoes. In this regard, Aurel felt immense solidarity with the Guineans, whose loyalty to classical elegance was unswerving. Whether they were wearing traditional clothing or European garments, the Africans showed flawless taste when it came to matching colors and to their choice of material. Aurel was all the more embarrassed to see his French compatriots so unworthy of their cultural heritage.

The commissaire greeted the deceased man's sister with the utmost respect. However, he seemed somewhat overexcited. After the usual welcoming formulas, he quickly announced: "We have some news about the investigation, Madame. Commissaire Bâ has called me; he's in charge of the investigation for the Guinean police."

Dupertuis gazed triumphantly around him. His coworkers quickly responded with a servile smile.

"Our Guinean friends have done a good job."

He wanted to add "for once," but restrained himself.

"This is what they've found out: a moneychanger at the black market in Cayah called them last night—these guys often work as informants, and they must have alerted him. He was presented with a five-hundred-euro note. That's very unusual around here."

"Where is Cayah?" asked Jocelyne Mayères.

"On the outskirts of Conakry, on the road to Sierra Leone."

Hanging on his office wall were a map of the country and a satellite view of the capital. Dupertuis now stood in front of them and pointed.

"It's here. So, the moneychanger called the police. He'd told his client to come back the next day, that an amount like that took time, etc."

Aurel remembered going that way once with Baudry on a sordid errand regarding a French citizen, a young backpacker who'd been robbed and held prisoner by a gang. As the young man's father had an important position with the Banque de France, the consul general felt he had to intervene personally. The neighborhood had a bad reputation. During the entire drive, Aurel got the feeling that Baudry had taken him along to serve as a human shield for him. In the end, everything went well.

"Commissaire Bâ, with whom we collaborate closely . . ."

As Dupertuis said "closely," he squeezed his fist, and the

gesture implied control more than collaboration. In any case, that was his notion of cooperation with the Africans: he conceived of it as being friendly and paternal, by virtue of an implicit hierarchy that placed the French police well above those they introduced as their "counterparts."

"As I was saying, Commissaire Bâ had the right reaction. He's a man of worth, a graduate of the prestigious police academy for criminal affairs in Lyon. He set a trap for the individual who wanted to change the five hundred euros. This morning at dawn—that was the time arranged by the moneychanger for the transaction—Bâ and his men took up their positions in the neighborhood. Unfortunately . . ."

Jocelyne Mayères was hanging on the policeman's every word. Aurel already knew what was coming. He turned his head and stared out the window.

". . . probably some sort of misstep. Unless the guy had an accomplice and he noticed some suspicious movement. When the man came in sight of our team, he smelled a rat and beat a hasty retreat. One of the members of Bâ's team tried to cut him off. The man pulled out a gun and shot the policeman."

"Was he killed?" exclaimed Jocelyne.

"He was wounded. But it's quite serious. They brought him to Conakry and operated on him this morning. He was shot in the stomach. I've just learned that he's out of danger."

"Did anyone recognize the aggressor?" asked Aurel, casually, because he already had an idea.

"An excellent question, M'sieur le Consul."

This casual way he had of pronouncing his title was a friendly sign to Aurel from the commissaire. A way of saying that between themselves they mustn't take notions of hierarchy too seriously, but each must continue, all the same, to play his respective role.

"That's the only positive thing about the whole failed operation. The man has been identified. He's a petty criminal who occasionally works as an informant, and several policemen recognized him."

Aurel very nearly cried out "Lamine," but caught himself in time.

"His name won't mean anything to you," said the commissaire, punctiliously. "A certain Lamine Touré. But that's not the most important thing. The Guinean police went back to his house. They'd had a quick look there after the murder, when they were combing the seedy neighborhoods for clues. They didn't find anything. This time they dug a little deeper. And they found out—"

"That he's the boyfriend of the infamous girl my brother was living with on his boat."

Overwhelmed by the trip and all this new information, Jocelyne Mayères could no longer make a clear distinction between the things Aurel had found out on his own and what she was already supposed to know.

"What? You already knew?"

A glance at Aurel was enough for her to realize she'd slipped up. He was nervously running a finger inside his shirt collar, as if he were trying to remove a tire from its rim.

"We found out this morning," stammered Aurel, looking at the commissaire. "That's actually what we were coming to tell you."

"And how did you find out?"

"Gossip. The assistant who works with me . . . you know, Hassan . . . he heard something yesterday in the shared taxi on his way home. People talk a lot there. A rumor. Just a rumor. Which is why we wanted to ask you about it . . ."

The commissaire gazed a moment longer at Aurel, flashing him the dark look he reserved especially for suspects. Then, once he'd decided to take him at his word, at least for today, he went on with his story, turning to Jocelyne Mayères.

"I am able—completely confidentially, of course—to confirm this rumor. The little gangster is indeed the girl's lover."

He coughed and tried to drum up some courage, looking at his colleagues one by one.

"Madame, I fear we must now deal with matters that are, shall we say, embarrassing, regarding your brother's life."

"Go ahead, please."

"Well, this young woman had been living with him for several weeks."

"I know."

"Already, this is a somewhat delicate matter, because according to what Monsieur le Consul has told us, your brother is married—"

"Separated."

"Fine. Whatever the case may be, it is not up to us to judge. However, the fact remains that this girl is what we commonly refer to as—"

"A prostitute."

In her desire to be helpful, Jocelyne Mayères was making the commissaire very uncomfortable, because he was actually looking for a word that would be less blunt.

"Not exactly. Not according to the meaning we might give the word in Europe. Let's just say that she was not—how to put it—disinterested."

"And the man who wounded the policeman was her pimp?"

By taking a questioning tone, she was saving Aurel's life. He looked at her, his face transfigured by gratitude.

"Most likely. Very likely, even."

The commissaire went and sat back down at his desk. His hands joined under his chin, he marked a pause, a sign that he was about to utter an important conclusion.

"These developments corroborate the theories we'd come up with on the basis of logical deductions. The crime was indeed committed by a handful of unsavory natives, acting in a coordinated manner. The girl won your unfortunate brother's trust and must have been sent to prepare the terrain. Her pimp joined her on the boat. We now know that he has a weapon. He killed Monsieur Mayères, and she gave him the key to the safe. Then she made it look as if she had been attacked."

Aurel felt like crying out, "And the mast? Why did they hang him from the top of the mast?" but he held his tongue and let Madame Mayères speak.

"What will happen now?"

"Well, Madame, we must hope our Guinean friends will prove efficient. A description of the guy has been sent to all the gendarmeries and border posts. All we can do now is wait."

"And the girl?"

"They're interrogating her again. I think they won't go easy on her. That much you can be sure of, with the Guineans. They went through enough suffering during the dictatorship to know how to make suspects talk."

Jocelyne Mayères looked astonished. The commissaire wondered if he was dealing not only with a grieving sister but also a human-rights activist. He hastened to amend his words:

"What I mean is, obtain a confession from the culprit. Perfectly legally, with respect for the rights of the defense, naturally."

"Naturally," echoed Aurel.

He had a fleeting image of Ceauşescu's jails, where he'd had the unhappy privilege of being detained several times, accused of "antisocial behavior."

The interview, as far as Dupertuis was concerned, was over. He was about to get up, but Jocelyne Mayères stopped him.

"Two or three things, Commissaire, if you don't mind."

"Why, of course . . . I am completely at your disposal, Madame."

"First of all, I would like to see my brother's sailboat."

"That shouldn't be difficult: there is always someone on guard. Commissaire Bâ will be happy to organize that for you."

"And I would like Monsieur le Consul to accompany me."

Aurel, who hadn't expected a thing, turned abruptly in his chair toward Jocelyne Mayères. He was extremely emotional in his dealings with women. For him, gratitude was the finest of feelings. God knows his wife had reproached him often enough for the humble-servant attitude he had displayed toward her. She'd thought it was ridiculous, but he couldn't help it. He needed to reach out to an all-powerful female entity and cover her hands in grateful kisses. The vague sympathy he had felt up to now for Mayères's sister was immediately transformed into an infinite debt which made him, now and forever, her slave and herald.

"If you like," said Dupertuis, casting a ribald glance at Aurel.

"Thank you, Commissaire. And one other thing."

"Yes?"

"I would like to meet that woman . . ."

"The girl who was on board the boat? You won't find out anything from her. She's a little slut; there are plenty of her kind here, hanging around with Europeans. It's all about money, you understand . . ."

"I don't care who she is. You see, my brother loved her."

"Loved her!"

A little smile lit up the policemen's faces. They gave each other knowing glances.

"In any case, he trusted her enough to take her on board and live with her. I would like her to tell me about him, about his last months."

No one was laughing anymore. They were all looking at this tall, serious woman who was speaking to them, observing them one after the other with her dark eyes wide open, unblinking.

"You know, Commissaire, several years ago I lost touch

with my brother. I would like to have something of his to keep, something about his life, to understand him better—"

"I'll see with the Guineans," interrupted the commissaire, fearful of succumbing to his emotions. "The car will take you back to your hotel, and I'll let you know as soon as I've been able to reach Commissaire Bâ."

Jocelyne Mayères stood up, very dignified. She held her hand out across the desk to the policeman. He took hold of it and kept it in his while he walked around the desk and stood before her.

"Thank you for your cooperation, dear lady."

It was as if he would have liked to conclude his elegant formula by kissing her hand, if it were something he was in the habit of doing. He walked over to the door and let the visitor go past him.

"Do you mind if I keep Monsieur le Consul a few minutes longer?"

"Not at all. I'll wait by the entrance. I have to call my husband."

"We won't be long."

The commissaire closed the door. Aurel was afraid he might be in for a reprimand, because of his closeness with Madame Mayères. He was afraid, above all, that Dupertuis might bring up the business about the rumors again, and the connection between Mame Fatim and Lamine. But the policeman had something else on his mind.

"Tell me, Aurel. Since you're in charge while Baudry is away."

In charge . . . there was still Lemenêtrier to reckon with. Never mind, thought Aurel.

"Here's the thing: we would like to have an autopsy done on Mayères, but nothing has come of it so far. I asked the Guineans. They eventually told me they don't have the means to pay for one. You know the state of their finances. They need

our help. It's not so much the autopsy in itself that is of interest, but it will allow us to take toxicological samples, and to
analyze the bullet, should they find it in the body. We have to
compare it with the bullet removed from the wounded policeman's abdomen. There's no lab here. We'll have to send it to
Dakar. More expense. Can the consulate release any funds? He
is a French citizen, after all."

"Certainly, certainly."

Aurel was relieved. Nothing serious, really. He could easily
find the funds in the consulate's budget; they always kept a
reserve for this sort of intervention. And thanks to his role as
financial overseer, he would be able to stay in the loop. They
couldn't withhold information about the outcome of these
investigations.

"I'll find out as quickly as I can."

Aurel was already at the door. But the telephone rang, and
he paused.

"Oh, it's you, Bâ!" shouted the commissaire into the
receiver.

At first he listened to what his Guinean counterpart had to
say. Aurel decided it would be better to wait before leaving the
room.

"In fact, I have the dead man's sister here with me, Madame
Jocelyne. Yes . . . she would like to see her brother's boat. Can
you let your guard know? Can she go there right away?
Perfect. No, I won't be going with her. She'll be with Aurel, the
consul. You met him in my office. Thank you. And when will
you be coming to see me? I have some good news about the
autopsy. Right away? Okay, I'll be expecting you."

He hung up and motioned to Aurel to leave.

"Go find your *belle dame*. You can leave for the marina
right away."

Aurel thanked him and reached for the handle of the
padded door.

"Off you go, lover boy!" said the commissaire with a wink.

Aurel flushed and fled, to the great delight of the three policemen.

* * *

"It's really very kind of you to let me come along. Thank you."

Squeezed in the back of the consular Clio, Aurel was feeling so emotional that he had waited until they were nearly there before saying these words. Jocelyne Mayères shrugged.

"What are you thanking me for?" she said, getting out of the car. "I trust you, that's all."

This compliment finished him off and destroyed any remaining courage he might have for a reply. He let the moment pass, then continued the discussion on a different front, where he might feel less sensitive.

"I called your sister-in-law."

"Oh, and how did she take it?"

"She told me she wouldn't be asking for anything. She didn't seem to be the least bit concerned about the succession."

"Aimée? You must be joking."

"No, I assure you. She was very dignified, and I got the impression I was hearing a woman who was pleased with her lot and wasn't expecting anything more."

"With all due respect, she was putting on an act. The way I know her, she would kill her own father and mother to get her hands on the fortune Jacques had accumulated."

"Would she kill her own husband, too?"

They looked at each other for a long while, in silence.

"If she showed no emotion at the thought that his fortune might have disappeared," Aurel said pensively, "maybe she knows where the money is to be found. And that it will go to her."

"Do you think that to get it she might have—"

"I don't think anything."

"I don't see how . . . from the Côte d'Azur, she could have got her husband killed."

"I don't, either."

"It seems totally implausible."

"'Those who believe in miracles are imbeciles; those who don't are atheists.' So my grandmother used to say, in Yiddish."

Jocelyne burst out laughing. Aurel was beside himself with happiness.

The car was going nowhere fast, because huge traffic jams paralyzed the capital every day at this time.

"Nor does your sister-in-law seem to be in any hurry to be informed of the outcome of the investigation. She won't be pressing charges. Do you want to?"

"My husband's a lawyer, and he advised me to. But it won't change anything for the time being. Except when dealing with terrorism, the wheels of French justice do not tend to turn quickly, and in any case it will take months. It's now that everything is at stake. If there's a chance to find out what happened to Jacques . . ."

She turned to Aurel, and, from the look she gave him, he understood that she was counting on him. He turned away to hide his emotion.

Fortunately, the car had reached the entrance to the marina. The driver dropped them off by the sidewalk. The heat was a little more bearable in the shade of the trees. Jocelyne took off her sandals and carried them by their straps. The sand along the path was soft and warm under her feet.

"What a lovely place."

"If you like the sea."

"You make me laugh, Aurel. You don't mind if I call you Aurel? We've become accomplices now, in a way. I'll be working with you on your little investigation . . ."

Aurel tried to make a sort of silent bow, and stumbled on a root.

Jocelyne, who was walking ahead, stopped at a spot where the path overlooked the marina.

"So, this is it?"

She had put her hands on her hips; her sandals were dangling next to her thigh. The sunlight shimmered on the smooth water of the marina. Aurel put on his dark glasses, and Jocelyne smiled as she looked at him.

"They're funny, those glasses of yours. You remind me of Yves Montand in *The Confession* . . ."

Aurel blushed and nervously stuffed the glasses in his pocket.

"Excuse me," he stammered.

The sailboats at their moorings were hardly moving. On their decks, canvas awnings were stretched between the masts and cast a colored shade. Under one of them, four people were just finishing lunch. A man in a swimsuit, his chest covered with dark hair, was smoking, leaning against a shroud. The whole place evoked vacation, but a special sort of vacation, without that impatience that often goes with it: a vacation that would never end.

"It's strange that Jacques would stay for so long in a place like this. He was so active . . ."

"Let's go find the boss first and say hello," Aurel managed to say, his mouth furry with emotion.

They headed toward the clubhouse. Three of the tables on the terrace had been occupied for lunch. Two of them were still laden with the dirty dishes and near-empty rosé bottles of a finished meal. At the third table, two elderly couples lingered, waiting for their coffees. Ravigot came out of the kitchen and grimaced when he saw Aurel and the woman with him. He set the cups down in front of his last customers and strolled unhurriedly over to the consul.

"Madame Mayères, allow me to introduce Monsieur Ravigot, the proprietor of this establishment."

Then, turning to Ravigot:

"Madame Jocelyne Mayères, the sister of the deceased man. She just got here yesterday, from France."

"Pleased to meet you, Madame. Allow me to offer my condolences."

Ravigot wasn't trying to be friendly. This whole business wasn't doing him any good. He was just waiting for it to be over, so he'd be left alone. He didn't like these constant developments.

"We've come to see the boat," said Jocelyne.

"Be my guest. I suppose the policeman on board has been notified?"

"Yes, yes."

"In that case, Seydou will row you out there. Seydou!"

Ravigot was glad of a chance to shout, in calling the caretaker. This allowed him to offload some of his bad mood. Unfortunately, Seydou must have been just behind the building. He stuck his head out the window, and Ravigot was deprived of the pleasure of more bellowing.

"Get out the skiff and take the lady and gentleman out to the *Tlemcen*."

Jocelyne and Aurel followed Seydou down to the pier.

"His boat is called the *Tlemcen*?"

"Yes, Madame," Seydou confirmed.

They climbed into the little skiff, and the caretaker rowed toward the sailboat.

Level with the water, the hum of the city was muted. What they heard, above all, was the refreshing sound of water lapping against the wooden bow. Cool air rose from the water. Jocelyne, at the fore, was watching how the hull of the sailboat grew larger as they drew closer.

"Where's the policeman?" asked Aurel, turning to Seydou.

They had reached the side of the sailboat, but no one appeared.

"He asked me to take him ashore an hour ago. When he heard there was going to be a visit, he took the opportunity to stretch his legs. There are two of them working twelve-hour shifts. In any case, they're not serving any purpose, and I don't think they'll keep them here much longer."

Seydou maneuvered the skiff next to an aluminum ladder at the stern of the sailboat. Jocelyne climbed nimbly on board. Aurel, still wearing his raincoat, hesitated when the time came to step across the space between the two boats. His right foot slipped and plunged briefly in the water. He let out a cry when he saw the fine leather swell with salt water.

Once he had fixed a mooring line around a rung in the ladder, Seydou climbed on board. The sailboat was much bigger than it appeared from the clubhouse. It measured roughly forty-five feet in length and had a wide beam to accommodate spacious cabins. The deck was tidy, with the exception of the main mast halyards, which had been hastily untied to lower the body.

"So, it's here that . . ." murmured Jocelyne.

Seydou pointed to the spreaders, and Aurel twisted his neck to look up.

"Yes, Madame. His feet were level with the little pulley you can see all the way at the top."

"Which means he was visible from a distance?" Aurel asked.

"At high tide, when the water comes as high as the sea wall, you can see the tops of the masts from all along the coast, outside the marina. Actually, the morning they found him, there were some curious sightseers who came from pretty far off because they saw the body when they opened their windows."

Jocelyne listened distractedly to these explanations. She had gone to the foredeck and was rubbing her fingers on the teak decking, where a spot of blood dried by the sun was visible. She was clearly upset; Aurel got the impression she was on the verge of tears.

"I'll sit here and wait," said Seydou. "You can have a look below. It's all open."

Aurel did not know what attitude to take at the sight of the emotion that had overcome Jocelyne. He said, "Would you like to go on your own or shall I come with you?"

"No, come with me, Aurel. Is this the way?"

Through a large opening, they could see a ladder and the gloom of the cabins. They went down one behind the other.

Nothing had been touched in the saloon. It was as if Mayères had not seen death coming. Dirty dishes were piled in the little sink, and lying on the table were newspapers, books, and even the half-moon glasses the deceased man must have worn for reading. They made their way toward the cabins on either side of a narrow passageway. Here, too, everything bore the mark of a presence. It was not so much untidy as lived-in; in the biggest cabin, the bed was covered with a blue fitted sheet, underneath a thin, crumpled top sheet. There were two pillows at the top of the bed, but only one seemed to have been used. Jocelyne sat down on the edge of the bed, and Aurel understood that she wanted to be alone with her thoughts. He continued his visit. A second cabin, next door, was in a great mess. Women's underwear was tossed on the floor and even on the ledge of the porthole. A heavy perfume of rose and musk lingered in the stuffy air. Aurel went out and quickly closed the door, as if it had been indiscreet to enter that female sanctuary. On the opposite side, another door opened onto an empty cabin. The bedspread had not been removed. Finally, at the very bow of the boat, Aurel tried to turn the knob of one last door, but he saw that the lock had been forced. When he opened the door he came upon a triangular cabin that had been fitted out as an office-cum-navigation station at the prow.

Shelves were stacked with nautical charts and navigation books. There were no documents on the table. This could be a sign of perfect tidiness, or the result of evidence having been taken by the police team. Under the desk, along the port-side wall, was a large combination and key safe. The door was wide open. Aurel got painfully down on all fours and peered into the open door. As the lack of light made it impossible to see inside properly, he felt around blindly with his hand. The safe was huge, with two levels. The upper level was empty. On the lower level, someone had shoved some papers all the way to the back which must not have interested them. Aurel methodically gathered them all up. When he stood up again, he placed what he'd found on the desk. They were piles of letters in order of year and bound together with string or raffia. There must have been thirty envelopes or more. The thief had ignored them, and so had the police. Aurel stuffed them into the big pocket of his trench coat.

He stayed for a moment longer in the cabin. Something seemed odd to him. He couldn't put his finger on it. He looked around and tried to fathom what it was that was bugging him.

The cabin was lit by a square hatch in the deck overhead. During the day, powerful sunlight came in through the hatch and lit up the space. Aurel could see in detail all the items—pens, notebooks, ink cartridges—that were lying along the edge of the workspace. He saw nothing abnormal about this. Suddenly he went closer to the wall. The hull of the boat was curved at this point, and each side of the cabin had the same rounded shape. So the wall was at a slant, curving in toward the flooring. Roughly twenty inches from the ceiling there was a little brass frame. In it was a photograph showing the *Tlemcen* in a harbor somewhere. This framed picture was the only decorative thing in the cabin. Aurel leaned closer to try and make out the figures standing on the deck of the boat, photographed while they were waving. It occurred to him that the picture might have been taken the day the sailboat was launched. He hunted among the blur of faces on the print to see if he recognized Aimée. There was not enough light on the picture, so Aurel grabbed it without thinking as if to bring it closer to his eyes. Just then, completely unexpectedly, the brass frame came loose from the wall and stayed in his hand. It had simply been clipped to the wall there to hide a horizontal copper plate that was screwed into the hull. The purpose of such an arrangement—which clearly had been made long after the boat was built—was mysterious. What would be the point of a narrow porthole like this? To let in more light? There was already plenty, and, in any case, the porthole had been blocked off. To let in air? The hatch in the ceiling could be opened wide. Aurel tried to remove the four large bolts holding the plate in place. They had hardly been tightened, and he managed easily. Then he pulled on the plate and realized that it was the thickness of the hull itself. Once he had removed it, he was left with a horizontal opening, almost level with the waterline. Aurel leaned closer and looked through the opening. He had a view of almost the entire marina. The sun had begun to set, and the occupants of the moored sailboats had removed their protective awnings. A woman was hanging laundry on a line. Two men were leaning over an outboard motor. Aurel closed the opening, tightened the bolts, and put the frame back in place.

Then he returned to Jocelyne, who had not left her brother's cabin. She had discreetly opened the cupboards, without removing anything, just to breathe in the cabin's particular atmosphere; it felt as if the occupant were about to come back at any moment.

"Look," she said, handing a frame to Aurel. "This is Jacques's daughter when she was six years old. Poor girl. And this is Robert, our older brother. The hero of the Algerian war, who was killed in Tlemcen."

On the rather blurry photograph, a young soldier was look-ing defiantly at the camera lens. On his head was a kepi with military stripes that he had put on at a slight tilt, a sign that he felt free enough in this uniform to wear it however he saw fit. Aurel couldn't see any resemblance in his features with Jacques Mayères, or with Jocelyne, for that matter. This soldier doomed to imminent death had a gentle, almost angelic expression; blond curls framed his face, and, despite the poor quality of the photograph, it was easy to conclude that his skin was soft and pink.

"There are reminders of Robert everywhere: his badges there, in the little box, a framed handwritten letter, and look what I found under the bed."

In her hand, she held a military helmet. On the interior, the straps were made of leather. When she turned it over, Aurel could see the perfectly round hole a bullet had left.

"One of his friends brought it to us after Robert's death. I couldn't remember what had become of it, this horrible hel-met. Jacques must have found it among our parents' things."

Aurel could tell how much this affected Jocelyne, and he didn't want to see her break down and cry. He felt he might easily cry with her. He took the object from her hand.

"Do you want to keep it?"

"No," she said. "Leave it here, under the bed or wherever."

She swung around and opened the door to the cabin.

"It's terrible, the burden we place on children sometimes. I have two kids, and I'm trying to keep them away from all this."

Without looking behind the other doors, she headed toward the salon, then back up on deck, where Seydou was waiting for them.

"Anything else you want to see?" he asked Aurel.

"Thank you. We can go back now."

They climbed into the skiff. Seydou cast off and reached for the oar to start rowing.

"Before we head back to shore, I'd like to go all the way around the boat, if you don't mind."

Jocelyne was too absorbed by her thoughts to question Aurel's little whim. Seydou maneuvered the skiff to stay close to the *Tlemcen's* side; he had to go further from the prow to avoid the anchor chain immersed in the water, then he came back down the other side. All around the hull, an orange line had been painted to separate the area above the surface of the water, painted white, from that below, which was black. This orange stripe, in its way, represented the waterline.

"Go a bit closer."

Upon Aurel's request, Seydou rowed the skiff up against the hull of the sailboat. You had to be right up close to make out, in the thickness of the orange line, the contour of the little horizontal porthole that opened into the nav station. The cover that Aurel had put back in place completely blocked it off, and had he not seen the opening from the inside, it would have been impossible to imagine that it existed.

They finished their trip around the boat, and Seydou turned his skiff toward the landing pier.

"Tell me one thing, Seydou. Why did Monsieur Mayères anchor his boat so far away from the others?"

"I don't know, but he's the one who chose the spot. One time the boss tried to make him move, because we were supposed to accommodate a very long sloop, but he refused, and we had to find another solution."

Back on land, they climbed into the Clio without stopping off at the clubhouse, and Jocelyne asked to go back to the hotel. She wanted to get some rest and probably some quiet time to think after this emotional experience. On the way over, Aurel told her about the discovery he'd made in the nav station.

"I don't know the first thing about boats," she said. "Is that usual, a little opening like that?"

"I don't think so. Besides, apparently your brother wanted it to remain discreet, or even secret."

"What do you think it means?"

"That he was afraid."

"Of who?"

"The *Tlemcen* was anchored in such a way that he could observe all the other boats through that little opening."

"And what's your conclusion?"

"That the danger was not inside the boat."

VII

At the hotel, there was a message from the commissaire. It was to inform them that the meeting with Mame Fatim had been approved. Jocelyne had until six o'clock that evening to go to the central commissariat. After that, the young woman would be transferred to the court to be presented to a judge.

"I'll have them drive you there right away," said Aurel.

"I'd like for us to go together. Please."

"But I don't think the commissaire—"

"Don't worry. I'll take care of it. Come."

Aurel was overwhelmed by this further sign of trust. It was clear, now, that they were conducting the investigation together. Very moved, he wedged himself in the back of the Clio. The only fly in the ointment: he was dying of thirst. With all this emotion he would gladly have drunk a large, cool glass of white wine. He'd been thinking about it all the way to the hotel. And now that they were leaving the place, he was still thinking about it.

The police headquarters were located in the center of town. The sidewalks in this neighborhood were overrun by crude market stalls, and itinerant merchants walked around waving all sorts of items, from hairdryers to Spiderman costumes, children's swim rings to tool kits.

Aurel cleared a path to the entrance for Jocelyne. The two policemen on guard let them in without saying a thing. Inside, a labyrinth of little corridors, stairways, and elevators brought them to the offices of Commissaire Bâ, but only after they had asked their way half a dozen times.

African administrative hierarchies have their own codes. One of them, perhaps the most important one, is temperature. The higher up an individual is in the pecking order, the colder their office. In the corridors there reigned a heat that came not only from outside but also from air conditioners, discharging the hot air extracted from private offices into the very place where the subordinates went about their business. Jocelyne Mayères was perspiring profusely. Halos of sweat darkened her shirt under her arms and around her neck. Aurel, still cinched tight in his raincoat, felt slightly unwell, despite his resistance. The only effect the heat had on him was to cause a tiny droplet to pearl on his temple.

Finally they reached the commissaire's offices. Two women wearing the same dark blue boubou were typing away at anti-quated computers. A tiny air conditioner lowered the temperature by a few degrees compared to the corridor. When the commissaire had been notified and the visitors were led into his office, it was as if they had suddenly changed continents. A glacial wind blew through the room, churned out by the wide open vents of three refrigerating machines.

Bâ was a tall, slender man, as Fula people often are. There was a simplicity about his person, one might even call it a sense of clarity, that was reflected in the décor. The room was painted white, and the mahogany desk was bare of any papers. Hanging on the walls were various diplomas from police academies in France, the United States, and Qatar. A Guinean flag, with its pole, was fixed to the wall by two nails.

The commissaire, who had adopted a humble and timid attitude toward his counterpart Dupertuis at the French embassy, was now in a position to behave majestically. He invited Jocelyne to sit down on the Havana leather sofa. Clearly, he didn't really know what to do with Aurel. He had expected him to go back out once he had delivered his com-patriot into safe hands. But when Aurel settled into one of the armchairs around the coffee table, Bâ didn't dare say any-thing.

"You haven't changed your mind, Madame? You still want to meet her face-to-face, this woman who—we are now con-vinced of it—helped to murder your brother?"

"More than ever, Commissaire."

"In that case . . ."

Bâ stood up and went to his desk. He pressed a button on the telephone and gave an order. Then he came and sat back down.

"I hope she won't behave badly with you. You see, she has something of a reputation, and even if Monsieur Mayères did . . ."

He could not find the words to continue without being offensive. They all fell silent for a long while, listening in spite of themselves to the din of the air conditioners. Finally there was a knock on the door. The commissaire gave the order to come in.

Two short policemen stood on either side of a tall young woman who was walking between them, anything but willingly. She was wearing a boubou she'd put on in a hurry, so it revealed her shoulders and the tops of her breasts. Bâ stood up precipitously and went over to adjust her clothing.

"Go sit down," he ordered, pointing to the empty leather armchair across from the others.

Mame Fatim sat gingerly on the edge of the seat.

"And try to answer properly."

The girl shrugged her shoulders. She was staring vacantly into space.

"Madame is Jacques Mayères's sister," Bâ announced, pointing to Jocelyne.

On hearing this, the girl's gaze lit up. She stared for a long time at the Frenchwoman, as if searching her face for familiar features.

And then there was a little incident. Mame Fatim leapt forward and fell to her knees at Jocelyne's feet. She wanted to take her hand, but her wrists were bound by handcuffs. As soon as she realized this, she began waving them frantically in every direction. Bâ and the two policemen rushed to grab her.

"I didn't kill him, Madame! I had nothing to do with it!"

Mame Fatim screamed while they dragged her back.

Once she was seized around the waist and made to sit back in her armchair, her chest shaking with sobs, it was Jocelyne who went over and took her hands.

"I believe you. Tell me what happened."

Bâ began to feel sorry he'd agreed to this confrontation. These *toubabs* really were incredibly naïve, and now this worthless girl was going to make them swallow any old rubbish. He stayed on the defensive.

"Had you known Jacques for long?"

"Almost two months."

Jocelyne was peering into Mame Fatim's face. She noticed her plump cheeks, sensual lips, fine nose, and the smooth copper of her skin, which seemed so soft.

She wondered what Jacques had loved about this woman. She could not bring herself to accept the idea that he might have just seen her as flesh to be consumed, sold, subjected. He was too sensitive a man for that.

"I had no reason to hurt him," murmured Mame Fatim, as if reading Jocelyne's thoughts. "He was always so kind to me."

She began weeping again, and Jocelyne, with one knee propped on the cushion of the armchair, began stroking her hair. Bâ exchanged a dismayed look with his men.

Aurel watched the scene, calling upon all his senses. He was moved by Jocelyne's reaction. But more than anything, he was making a huge effort to concentrate and observe every one of

Mame Fatim's expressions, to detect the slightest sign of hypocrisy or duplicity.

Suddenly the young woman sat up straight, grabbed Jocelyne's arm with both hands, and gazed at her, her eyes misting over with tears.

"I swear to you, Madame, I didn't kill him."

"I know you went off with your boyfriend that night. What time did you get back?"

"Ah, you know about that. Well, yes, I did go into town with Lamine," she confessed unworriedly, to the great astonishment of Bâ and his men.

She had not told them about this escapade.

"Did you do that often?"

"Several times a week."

"I suppose that depended on whether Lamine was free?"

The commissaire was increasingly surprised to discover how much Jocelyne knew.

"Yes," said Mame Fatim, sniffling.

"Was Jacques aware of this?"

"In the beginning, it's true, I didn't tell him anything. But he eventually figured it out."

"And he didn't mind?"

"You see, Jacques was a good man. He didn't want to live alone, and he was happy just having someone live with him on his boat. He wanted to do me a favor."

She wiped her tears and sat up straighter.

"He had plans for me," she said, with a burst of pride that was touching. "He wanted me to get an education. In the evening he gave me lessons in English and math. I didn't always understand a lot, but he was patient."

A brief spasm of nervous laughter shook her.

"I think he looked on me kind of as his daughter."

"Apparently you put sleeping tablets in his glass so that you could go out."

"That'll be Seydou who told you that. I made up a story to tell him because he saw me leaving with Lamine: I had to give him an explanation. If I had told him that Jacques knew about it, he wouldn't have understood the situation. He would have looked down on Jacques. You don't know what it's like, the honor code among Fulas . . ."

"So you didn't give him sleeping pills? But they were found in his cabin."

"Very rarely. He'd had a small heart episode. In the evening, I prepared his medicine for his blood pressure. He took it and went to bed and wished me good night. It's true there were times when I felt he was really tense, so I put a sleeping pill in, too. He knew I was going out, but all the same, it was easier if he was asleep."

"Did you give him any the night he died?"

"That day, I don't know why, he'd been on edge all day long. I'd never seen him like that. In a real panic. He kept trying to call someone, and apparently they weren't answering. He went back and forth between the deck and his office—the nav station at the front of the boat."

"Do you know what he was doing there?"

"No. I didn't go in there."

"So, before you went out, you gave him something to help him sleep."

"I told you, he was really tense. The night before, he hadn't slept a wink. He stayed shut inside the nav station. To be honest, he kind of scared me. I was afraid that at the last minute, he might do something . . . you know what I mean? Or, at least, that he wouldn't let me leave. Lamine was waiting for me, and if I didn't show up, he might come and get me. And then what would've happened? Actually, I wanted to protect Jacques. So I didn't say anything, but I put something in his glass."

Bâ was increasingly astonished. Previously, Mame Fatim

had answered all his questions, not hiding anything, but he realized he hadn't asked the right ones.

"Why did you steal his money, if you had so much respect for him?" the commissaire interrupted.

Because Mame Fatim, while she might deny having anything to do with the murder, had confessed that with her help Lamine had forced open the safe. She gave a shrug and turned back to Jocelyne instead.

"If you only knew, Madame . . . ever since I met Jacques, Lamine was constantly telling me to give him the combination to the safe. Lamine's a crook. And he's stubborn. When he wants something, he doesn't let go. We fought a lot. He even hit me. To him, Jacques was a *toubab* like all the others, a pile of gold, that was all. I tried to make him understand—"

"And finally you gave in, and the two of you killed him," said the commissaire.

Mame Fatim turned abruptly to him and shouted, "No!" The two policemen behind her were already rushing forward to seize her.

"Let her finish," said Jocelyne. "So, on the night in question, you went out. And then?"

"And then Lamine brought me back at around five in the morning. We started rowing out to the boat. There was no moon. It was pitch dark. We only saw the body at the very last moment. I nearly cried out, but Lamine put his hand over my mouth."

"You knew right away that it was Jacques?"

"No. Lamine maneuvered the rowboat right next to the hull. He put one of the two oars inside our boat and used the other to move forward slowly. We stayed like that for a long time, holding our breath and looking up, trying to understand."

"Was anyone still on the boat?"

"That's what we were trying to find out. But we didn't hear

a sound. And once our eyes adjusted to the dark, we saw that it was Jacques hanging up there, and that he was dead."

"Why didn't you tell us any of that?" the commissaire interrupted.

And, turning to Jocelyne:

"She told us that Lamine got on board and forced her to give him the combination to the safe, and that he went away again once he'd tied her up, without waking Mayères."

Mame Fatim bristled, like a cat sensing a threat.

"You didn't know that I went out at night with Lamine," she spat, "so I wasn't about to tell you."

It was obvious that when they were beating her she had confessed as little as possible, to diminish her own role in the affair. And that had sufficed for the policemen. In any case, they had already made up their minds. They were hardly about to credit the testimony of a girl like that.

"Go on," Jocelyne said gently.

"When we realized that Jacques was dead and the murderers were gone, Lamine said, 'See, not everyone is as stupid as we are.' He was sure they had killed the *toubab* to rob him."

"And you, what did you think?"

"I was scared. I figured they would accuse me. I told Lamine we should run away."

"And he refused?"

"He said, 'Wait. Let's just make sure.' So we climbed on board and went to the cabin where the safe is. Then we saw that it was intact."

"And so you opened it," Jocelyne asked softly.

"How could I refuse? Jacques was dead. Lamine was there next to the safe."

"And you had the combination?"

"It was a fairly simple safe, according to Lamine. It opened with a key, and I knew where Jacques kept it."

"And what did you find inside?"

"I don't know exactly. Lamine sent me up on deck to keep a lookout. When he came up, he seemed pretty annoyed. He said, 'Are you sure there's not another one?'"

"What did he expect to find?"

"We used to talk about Jacques a lot. Lamine would ask me questions. How he sold his company, did he have stocks at the bank, how much could he have brought with him . . . all that. He came to the conclusion that he must have brought his fortune with him."

"And in actual fact?" asked the commissaire.

"Lamine put everything that interested him into a little plastic bag. It didn't amount to much."

"In five-hundred-euro notes, it can add up quickly," said Bâ with a scornful smile.

"There was a gun, too, with two boxes of ammunition. Lamine put them in his jeans pockets."

"Why didn't you run away with him?" asked Jocelyne.

"I wanted to. I was scared to death. But Lamine told me we wouldn't make it, if there were two of us. I think he mainly wanted to go on his own."

"So you were okay with that?"

"He didn't give me any choice. He pushed me into the cabin and slapped me. My head was ringing. He tied me up on the bed and told me to say I'd been raped. I began shouting. He came back from the kitchen with a roll of masking tape and stuck a piece over my mouth. That was it."

Mame Fatim had finished her statement, and a heavy silence fell in the room.

Jocelyne did not take her eyes off the girl. In a gesture of tenderness, she stroked her chin. The commissaire could not stand this much credulity.

"I wouldn't give too much credence to the stories this girl's been telling you, Madame. She wants to cover for her boyfriend and save her own skin. We have every reason to believe that there are not two separate perpetrators in this affair. Whoever committed the theft also committed the murder."

He continued to put forth his arguments, but no one was listening anymore. The two women looked at each other in silence, and Aurel, leaning forward, continued to focus on the young woman's face.

* * *

"What do you think?"

Aurel had his glass of white wine at last. And he was even enjoying the luxury of a smoke, because Jocelyne had noticed him fiddling with his cigarette holder and not daring to take it out of his pocket. They were sitting at a table in the courtyard of a little restaurant run by a Frenchwoman. Fascinated by Morocco, the proprietress had hung large triangular canvases above the tables, painted the walls red ocher, and put up Berber mirrors here and there. The place was a sanctuary of tranquility and relatively cool air in the heart of the old town. It was early afternoon, and all the customers had already left. Jocelyne and Aurel, sitting in a corner near a gurgling wall fountain, could speak at leisure without any fear of being overheard.

"I think she's telling the truth. While the two of you were speaking, I didn't take my eyes off her. Life has taught me how to tell when people are being sincere. At times it's been a question of life or death for me. This girl? I trust her."

"So do I."

They sat for a long while pensively turning their glasses, the sides pearling with a cool dew.

"Aurel, tell me something . . ."

"Yes?"

"What drove you to carry out this investigation all on your own?"

"I'm not all on my own. We're in it together."

His words had come out too quickly. He blushed, for fear they might be misinterpreted. His passion for Jocelyne was a mixture of admiration, gratitude, and respect. To him she was like a knight's lady. He would have been very embarrassed if she thought anything else.

He continued, speaking very quickly.

"When I first got to France, I dreamt of being a policeman. It's idiotic, you might say. Maybe, but you have to understand that back then, in communist Romania, the only films we got from the West were either adventure or police films. We grew up with Belmondo and Delon. I didn't think I had any chance of becoming an adventurer like *That Man from Rio*."

"Why not?"

"You're too kind, Jocelyne. But don't try to make me believe you haven't noticed."

"Noticed what?"

"That I don't exactly have Belmondo's looks."

"You feel closer to Alain Delon, then?"

They laughed, even if deep inside, Aurel was slightly hurt by her question.

"To be a policeman, you see, it's something else that matters: logic, skill in evaluating people, being able to penetrate different milieus."

"Then why didn't you go through with it, in the end?"

Aurel finished his glass and waved to the waiter to bring two more.

"When I arrived in France, my family, who'd paid to get me out of Romania, didn't have the means to support me. I had to start earning a living right away. I tried giving piano lessons, but I couldn't make much with that. And I hadn't got very far in my classical training. So I began playing in bars."

"In bars?"

Aurel noticed Jocelyne's expression: he saw that she'd spotted his little lie.

"Well, bars, you know what I mean. Nightclubs with girls, champagne, and clients who don't really go there for the music."

"I see."

"So when I finally went one day to a police station to tell them I wanted to work for them, it didn't take long for the guy interviewing me to figure out who he was dealing with. A Romanian refugee who plays the piano at night in—"

"Brothels."

Aurel was sincerely sorry to have brought his Lady Jocelyne down to such a vulgar level.

"Anyway. This is not a conversation for a woman like you."

Jocelyne smiled as she watched her funny little companion grow flustered and squirm in his seat in search of another topic. She decided to tease him.

"If I've got this right, you can't be a cop if you've been a pianist in a sleazy bar, but you can be a French consul."

Aurel felt unbearably awkward, which was visible from the grimace on his face and the nervous little bouncing motion he made in his chair.

"I'm wasting your time with my life story."

"Not at all. It interests me."

"Really?"

Aurel regained a bit of courage and sipped the last drops of his white wine. The waiter, who had been watching the scene from a distance, brought him another glass, unasked.

"It's fairly straightforward, actually. Everything began . . . the evening when . . . how can I explain this?"

"Go ahead."

"The day . . . I closed the piano."

There was so much gravity in the way he said this that Jocelyne couldn't help but burst out laughing.

"You see, what's the point in me telling you," said Aurel, looking vexed.

"No, forgive me. It's just the way you said it. So you were saying, you closed the piano?"

"Yes, at a nightclub. It was three in the morning, and I was playing a piece by Duke Ellington. I remember it like it was yesterday. Three guys were drinking and smoking around the piano. There was this girl there, too, going from one guy to the next. My instructions were to play without stopping, as if I didn't notice anything. That's what I did, but suddenly one of the guys began to retch, and then he threw up. This story is horrible, forgive me."

"Go on. I still don't see what any of this has to do with your career as a diplomat."

"Of course," said Aurel, forcing himself to smile. "I have to start with this because it's important for what comes next."

"I see."

Aurel felt like shrugging. Clearly, she didn't understand. She couldn't understand. No one could. He suddenly wished he could cut the story short.

"It was no big deal, obviously. But somehow it was the beginning of everything. I stopped playing and didn't move. Everyone in the bar was looking at me. I was sitting stock-still, and . . . crying."

"You were crying?"

"I don't know what was going on in my head. I was completely disheartened. Up to then, I'd put up with everything without losing hope—communism, prison, exile, poverty, odd jobs. I'd lost touch with my family, the country I'd grown up in—however horrible it might have been—and for what, in the end? To come to this point. In that cesspool. Do you see, Jocelyne?"

Fatigue, emotion, and white wine had gotten the better of his guile; he had called Jocelyne by her first name, and if the waiter hadn't arrived just then with their food, he might even have grabbed her hand and buried his face in it, sobbing.

"In short," he concluded, regaining his self-control, "I decided to change my life. I closed the piano, I stood up, and I walked out. I never went back to that or any other bar. I began giving private lessons again, and I was determined to die of starvation if I had to, but with my honor intact."

"How old were you?"

"Twenty-seven."

"And . . . your diplomatic career?"

"Oh, that was pure luck. I replied to a classified ad and made the acquaintance of a wonderful family. I was giving lessons to a young lady. To be honest, she was no longer what you'd really call a young lady. She was older than I was, almost forty, but she was pure, intelligent, and sensitive."

"And pretty?"

"In my eyes, yes. Others might have said she was a bit on the heavy side, and it's true she didn't make much effort in the fashion department. She also had warts on her chin and nose which she should've had removed. But things like that didn't bother her. Or me, either."

"And did you ask her to marry you?"

"Me? I wouldn't have dared. She was so superior, in my eyes, so inaccessible . . ."

"And so?"

"And so one day her father stopped me after the lesson and spoke to me. He asked me if I could conceive of . . . marrying his daughter. I was quite unnerved."

"You didn't have a girlfriend at the time?"

"None," protested Aurel.

"And in Romania?"

"Oh, I'd had a few bad experiences there. You know, to me, women are supernatural beings, infinitely precious. I had my mother and grandmother as my model: they were the driving force behind everything. They were the backbone of the family, and I thought the entire world must be like that, revolving around these atoms of grace and kindness we call women."

"Do you still believe that?"

"Alas, I've come to realize the world isn't like that. I know that exceptional women are rare. But I keep searching, and there are some."

Having said this, fearful that Jocelyne might yet again take it as too emphatic an allusion, he became awkward and hastily continued his story, in a hoarse voice.

"My future father-in-law was a diplomat. He had just retired, but he still had a lot of connections at the Ministry of Foreign Affairs. He told me that once I was married to his daughter, he was sure he'd be able to obtain French nationality for me fairly quickly. Then I would have to take a little test, a mere formality. Not even three years later, I obtained my first position at a consulate."

"And . . . your wife?"

"She's in France," said Aurel glumly.

"She doesn't go with you when you're posted abroad?"

Aurel took a bite of his food, chewed it solemnly, and wiped his mouth.

"It would take too long to explain. Let's just say we never had a real life together. Our personalities are very different. Marriage came late in life for her. Her parents insisted, but she preferred to continue with her solitary habits. And the posts I received didn't appeal to her. The first one was in Niger, in the Sahara—Zinder, to be exact. I don't know if you're familiar with the place?"

"No."

"Well then, allow me to spare you the pleasure. Sand, dust, intolerable heat, and now there are terrorists . . ."

"Did you get divorced?"

"Yes."

Aurel sighed. For a long while they sat eating their white

grouper in silence, pulling out the bones. Jocelyne decided it would be inhumane to pursue the subject any further, and she took another tack to resume the conversation.

"So, regarding my brother's death, what do we have, with this latest information? If the girl is telling the truth, someone else must've gotten there first. Who could it be?"

"Your brother was afraid, like I said. He was afraid of some danger from outside. Which begs the question: why did he stay in a place where he felt threatened? Unless he felt threatened everywhere, which would explain the round-the-clock surveillance device he'd installed in the hull of the boat."

"What will you do?"

"We have to think carefully. We still don't have enough to go on. Let's just suppose his wife thought she'd had a raw deal and did want to get her hands on the fortune, and she sent someone after him? That would be what I call constant danger."

"Knowing her, it's possible," said Jocelyne pensively.

"But in that case, why didn't the aggressors break into the safe, since the whole point was to get their hands on the money?"

"A pertinent question. Maybe they didn't have time. Maybe they got interrupted by the arrival of Mame Fatim and her boyfriend."

"But would they still have had time to hang him from the mast?"

"That's the part I really don't get."

They thought for a moment in silence, removing a few little fish bones stuck in their teeth.

"Now," Aurel continued, "this marina is a hub for drug trafficking. Let's suppose something else: that your brother saw something he wasn't supposed to see. Maybe he was afraid of reprisals. People who interfere are quickly eliminated in this context. That would be what I call local danger."

"If that was the case, could he have run away?"

"These mafias have relays all along the coast. Maybe he felt safer in this marina he knew rather than out on the open ocean or in an unfamiliar port."

"What do you plan to do?"

"Keep on looking," said Aurel.

He checked his watch.

"Actually, I have to get back to the consulate. My assistant should have some new developments for me by now. Then I'll go to the Legion of Honor dinner."

"So you're abandoning me?"

Aurel blushed right up to his ears. Jocelyne laughed to herself. It was so easy to get him flustered.

VIII

Hassan had done a good job. At Aurel's request, he'd gone to the Department of Maritime Affairs located near the port. As he wandered down the corridor, he eventually ran into another vague cousin. Family relations in Africa constitute an invisible fabric beneath the trompe-l'oeil décor of official institutions. An administrative director and a courier might have very close blood ties and do each other favors in a manner hardly imaginable from their visible hierarchical positions. Conversely, two apparently equal dignitaries might turn out to be divided by age-old conflicts, where one persists in viewing the other as a former vassal, or even a descendant of slaves. Hassan, however modest his position at the embassy, belonged to a noble Fula family whose members showed solidarity. The cousin who worked for Maritime Affairs was surprised and pleased to happen upon his relative in the corridor.

Aurel's instructions to his coworker were to find out as much as possible about the activity of the boats in the marina from the time Mayères arrived, six months earlier. In answer to his request, Hassan's cousin told him that the information provided by the ports in Guinea had been compiled on a computer file since 2008. Upon entry, every vessel was registered, with its country of origin, destination, and dates of arrival and departure. The sailboats in the marina were in a separate category within the same overall file. There was nothing particularly confidential about this information. The cousin had no objection whatsoever to printing out a copy for Hassan. Hassan took it back to the office, delighted.

Aurel found something else that heartened him when he got back to the consulate. In addition to the precious list Hassan gave him, he obtained some interesting information from the commissaire. Analysis of the bullets did indeed show that the bullet Lamine had fired at the policeman and the one that had killed Mayères were not the same caliber. The latter was a standard 9mm ammunition, whereas the one the criminal boyfriend had used seemed to belong to a fairly old and rare type of weapon. A French army pistol, for example, of the type used in Algeria.

For Aurel, this information corroborated Mame Fatim's version of events. Lamine must have found the weapon in Mayères's safe, along with some cartridges. He would have had no reason to take it if, like the sailor's murderer, he'd had a handy, modern 9mm at his disposal.

As for the autopsy, it revealed that Mayères had indeed ingested strong sleeping tablets that evening, but the dose was normal. The time of death was difficult to determine precisely and would not contribute anything decisive.

Aurel took note of all this information in a perfectly casual manner, in the course of a desultory conversation with the commissaire. The policeman was in a very good mood. He'd had news from France, where his son was a student. The boy had passed his exams and informed his father that he, too, wanted to join the police.

"You see, Aurel, I've always thought he was just like me."

With a recruit like that, those petty criminals had better watch out.

"Will you be at the Association of Merit ceremony tonight?" asked Aurel, adding a touch of respect to his tone.

Dupertuis was proud to rank as an officer of the Legion of Honor. This positioned him well above the other members, who'd had to bend over backwards to obtain their Order of Merit or, at best, the red ribbon of a Knight of the Legion of Honor.

"Marcelly bores me stiff with his association. Besides, if I go, they'll all come rushing over to find out how the investigation is going. I'd rather stay here and work. Are you going?"

The commissaire's question contained a note of indignation. He could not recall that Aurel had ever been honored by any such distinction. And, however friendly his feelings toward him, he couldn't help but think that Aurel wasn't worthy.

"Marcelly asked me personally to represent the consulate. I have no choice but to show up. But I won't stay long."

"In that case, you can tell me about it. Have fun with all those old fogeys!"

Aurel, chuckling loudly, made his way out. He left the room practically walking backwards. Dupertuis loved to see him grovel like this.

* * *

The colonial building known as l'Ancien Cercle was built according to the norms of comfort and majesty cultivated among late-nineteenth-century military men. At the time of its construction, it must have been surrounded by vacant lots and a few humble shacks; by looking out over this poverty, its elegant colonnade had sought to symbolize the authority of France and the benefits it promised to bring these primitive lands.

Unfortunately for its designers, the Roman era was long over, and the monument was not aging well. The columns were covered with cracked cement and peeling paint, and the stucco was falling off in slabs. The building had lost a great deal of its majesty. Various associations used it as a banquet hall. These associations met there after nightfall, and in the dim electric light the décor regained a touch of solemnity. Those who were most nostalgic for the colonial period could still catch the odd whiff of glory.

When Aurel walked in, the cocktail hour was in full swing. Mingling out on the terrace were military aid workers, biracial couples, pensioners dodging the tax man, and aging whites who had stayed on after decolonization, all holding flutes filled with sparkling rosé wine. The city had been developed all around Le Cercle, gradually reducing its territory. In former times, the terrace had overlooked the sea, and it had been possible to imagine the coast of France far beyond the horizon. But now the view was blocked not five yards away by a wall that, unfortunately, didn't stop the smells of fried food wafting up from the little street below.

Aurel didn't know many people there. If several people did look at him when he came in, it was above all because after several sleepless nights, the crown of curls around his balding head was wildly disheveled and made him look like a madman. He only realized when he walked past a mirror, and he tried to comb his hair with his fingers. Then he exchanged some words with one of the few guests he recognized, a retired military doctor by the name of Poubeau. Why had he settled in Guinea? No one knew, and Aurel certainly had no interest in finding out. He had met him once because of an ingrown toenail he'd had to have treated. Dr. Poubeau no longer practiced, but he'd kept all his instruments and occasionally did favors for members of the French community who didn't want to resort to the local hospitals.

Aurel had hoped to miss the speeches by arriving late. Unfortunately, just after he came in, Marcelly asked for silence and reached for a malfunctioning microphone, set up in a corner of the terrace.

For a long fifteen minutes, he indulged in a lyrical, patriotic description of Mayères, full of grating, flowery expressions.

There was not much to be learned from his verbiage, other than the fact that Mayères had approached Le Cercle as soon as he arrived in Conakry, that he'd attended regularly, and that he'd gratified its members with a brilliant presentation devoted to "the military reality of the Algerian war." Marcelly recalled that Mayères defended the theory much loved by the *pieds noirs*, according to which the war had been lost because of the intellectuals' treachery and De Gaulle's felony. He asserted that the army, given enough time and support, would have eventually crushed the rebellion and made it possible to keep Algeria as part of France.

For most of the people there that evening, this opinion sat well with deeply rooted political convictions. There were smiles of approval. Aurel thought this was probably a misunderstanding. Mayères, by defending the French army in Algeria, had been paying tribute to the futile heroism of his brother. He was not, for all that, convinced of the necessity of the war itself. To be sure, he supported the notion that victory might have been possible—but did he really believe it was desirable? How could he, this left-wing company owner, share the ideas of those who were nostalgic for the colonies and French Algeria? It's true that some people's minds can contain ideological contradictions and that human beings are full of ambiguities. All the same, it made you wonder.

Gradually losing the thread of the speech, Aurel began to look at the people around him. He imagined Mayères here among with them and couldn't shake off a certain malaise. Maybe he was wrong about Mayères, but he sensed that, in sum, the man had been sincere, disinterested, and even a bit foolhardy, which didn't tally with the affected gravity of these bourgeois notables. What had he come looking for here?

Marcelly's speech ended, and the audience began to return inside, where a buffet had been laid out. Aurel caught the sleeve of a waiter he knew and pleaded for a glass of white wine instead of sparkling. He waited out on the terrace.

Only a few smokers were still lingering outside. One of them, leaning on a column, recognized the consul and waved to him. Aurel went over. He was a civil servant in charge of the embassy's customs office, a small cell consisting of two French employees and one Guinean intern. The consulate occasionally had to make use of his services when it came to importing equipment. But it was well-known that he mainly handled drug-trafficking issues.

"A sad affair, isn't it?" said the man.

He was fairly short, and although he must have been over sixty, his hair was still thick and black. His deep-set gray eyes seemed to be waiting in ambush. He had the pinched lips of people who probably accomplished most of their efforts, including long manhunts, in silence. Aurel couldn't recall his name.

"Yes," he replied, "did you know him well, this Mayères fellow?"

"Fairly well."

"Do you belong to Le Cercle?"

"I come more or less regularly. There's not that much entertainment around here."

Aurel would not have spontaneously used the word "entertainment" to describe the activities of Le Cercle, but to each his own, after all.

"Since you're sort of connected with the police," said Aurel in a syrupy tone, "do you have any theories about who might have done the deed?"

The customs officer took a long drag on his cigarette and gave it some thought.

"No, I don't have a clue, and, anyway, I'm not with the police. But I've heard it said he had a lot of money on him. That's not really a good idea in a place like the marina."

The minute he said it, Aurel had a flash of recall: "Cortegiani." That was the name he'd been looking for. The customs officer's name was Cortegiani.

"That's right, you must know quite a bit about what goes on in that marina. Apparently it's a hub for drug trafficking."

Cortegiani crushed his cigarette on the ground. Aurel was afraid his interlocutor might head for the buffet now, too. But Cortegiani immediately lit another cigarette, and smoking wasn't allowed inside (a rare constraint in the country, which gave Cercle members the faint illusion of being in France). Two white wicker armchairs were free at the end of the terrace.

"Shall we have another drink out here?" suggested the customs man, signaling to the waiter.

When Aurel had mentioned the marina, he'd shot him a suspicious look. But it was a sort of professional tic. Aurel got the feeling that, beneath his fierce manner, there was really just a lonely man who wanted to talk.

"It's true," said Cortegiani.

The customs officer belonged to that category of conversational partners who digest things slowly. He was replying without any transition to the question Aurel had asked him about the marina, before they went to sit down at the end of the terrace.

"That's strange," said Aurel, to encourage him to elaborate. "We don't often hear about drug seizures around here."

The customs man took a long drag on his cigarette, and Aurel waited in vain for the smoke to re-emerge.

"The Guineans have a foot in both camps," he said at last.

"Oh?"

The waiter brought two more glasses. The customs man quenched his thirst before continuing his train of thought.

"They let us work, provided we don't arrest anyone on their territory. That way they get to have their cake and eat it, too."

"What do you mean by 'work'?"

Another dark gaze from Cortegiani, and Aurel was afraid he'd been too direct. The customs man took his time, puffing on his cigarette.

"The customs office does everything," he announced proudly.

He was holding his cigarette between thumb and index finger, looking at it the way he would have looked at a harmful creature he had finally trapped.

"The police, the secret service, the gendarmerie . . . they'll all tell you they're involved in the fight against drug trafficking. That's not true."

His two fingers had eventually strangled the filter on the cigarette. He raised it to his lips to suck out the last of its blood.

"It's customs," he added, as if he were intent on claiming responsibility for his crime.

Aurel thought he'd forgotten his initial question and was about to put it to him again, when his interlocutor startled him.

"You want to know what it means, work? Well, a lot of things, I can tell you. Quite a lot. I don't know what it's like at the consulate, but my department is very busy. Day and night. We don't get weekends or vacation. Opportunities to relax, like now, are rare. Very rare."

To Aurel, this laborious conversation seemed anything but relaxing. But he understood that Cortegiani must not get many chances to talk freely, and above all to highlight his own worth. Now, in Aurel, he'd found the ideal listener. Aurel was sufficiently ignorant about these topics to be easily impressed and, at the same time, was an embassy employee like Cortegiani himself, which freed the customs man from the caution ordinarily imposed by professional secrecy.

"Don't forget that we're fighting on every front: land, air, and sea. Those bastards don't know what to try next to get their goods past us."

He'd finished his glass much more quickly than Aurel, who was hardly slow in that department. The waiter, who must have known the customs man well, rushed to bring him another glass, along with a bowl of peanuts.

"If we take just the sea, for example, we have to gather data about shipments, and keep watch on the movements of suspicious vessels. That's what I mean by 'work,' you see: observing the crew's every little move, transfers of cargo, placing tags . . ."

He said these last words in a hush. And all at once, his paranoid gaze was trained on Aurel as if he were guilty by virtue of hearing a secret. At the same time, Aurel sensed that this was one of the secrets Cortegiani found the greatest pleasure in divulging.

"Tags?" echoed Aurel.

"Yes, little transmitters we can attach to the hull of a boat that allow us to follow it by satellite. Even if they switch off all their devices. Even if they think they're invisible . . ."

"How do you attach the tag?" asked Aurel, opening his eyes round and wide, as if he were perfectly naïve.

"We use divers, of course."

"You have divers in the customs office!"

"Ha, ha!"

After snickering, Cortegiani tossed his cigarette butt into the garden. He took a moment to reach for another pack, painstakingly tore off the cellophane wrapper, and opened it. He gazed at the little white cylinders all in a row, as if he were about to choose which one to take out. Then suddenly a thought came to him, and he held the pack out to Aurel.

"You see these cigarettes all lined up? I'll take the one I need. I'm the one who decides. Well, the customs office is the same thing. Imagine you have before you all the services of the state: the various police headquarters, information agencies, the army, combat divers, special forces, the gendarmerie, the air force . . . we use them if the need arises."

Like all civil servants, the customs officer was fond of this expression, but he saw more to it than mere linguistic usefulness. It was the very heart of his office's power. He must be obeyed "if the need arises." It was inconceivable to question what that need might be. That was where the obscure customs official found the reward for all his sacrifices. His humility, "if the need arose," was transformed into omnipotence.

Aurel understood that only one facial expression was appropriate: admiration. Very early in life, under the heel of Ceaușescu, he'd learned how to do this, knew how to put on the right face. The interlocutor had to be able to clearly detect surprise, approval, submission, and terror, in order to be assured of complete triumph.

Strains of music came from the building, louder whenever the waiters opened the doors. Marcelly must have given the signal, and the elderly Guinean man who had set up the buffet put a CD in the stereo. During a recent meeting of the association committee, they had decided to replace the accordion with rock music. It was less patriotic but easier to dance to, in the opinion of the "younger generation," those who'd turned twenty in the 1970s.

Cortegiani, who hadn't stopped smoking or drinking, had slumped down in his chair. After the victory he'd obtained over Aurel, by making him assess the invisible but supreme importance of his mission, he went back to his ruminating.

Aurel wondered if he could still get anything out of him, but Cortegiani didn't seem to hear his questions.

"And what about Mayères in all this? Did you meet him here or at the marina?"

Some guests had requested a tango, and the sound of the bandoneon reached the terrace, driving Cortegiani even further into his melancholy.

Suddenly the French doors were opened wide, and the music overwhelmed the space outside the building. The waiters had cleared away the scattering of chairs and placed them beneath the colonnades, in order to transform the terrace into a dance floor. Aurel and Cortegiani were able to stay where they were because they were off to the side, but their quiet interlude had clearly come to an end, and they would soon have to move on. Aurel had assumed the conversation was over, when suddenly Cortegiani turned to him with an unpleasant expression on his face.

"I met Mayères here," he said, his voice muffled, but his face pressed up to Aurel's, who heard him distinctly. "Here, you understand? Nothing to do with the marina. Did you hear me?"

He kept his gaze fixed for a long while on Aurel, as if he were in a boxing ring, making sure his opponent was out for the count.

Then he stuffed his pack of cigarettes into his pocket and, grunting a "good night" that required no response, he disappeared like a shadow into the garden.

* * *

Aurel left Le Cercle feeling quite sloshed. And yet he hadn't drunk half as much as the customs man. It was at times like this that he missed Europe the most. In Paris, he would have walked home, and that would have sobered him up. Walking also helped him think, and he needed more than ever to get some clarity in his thoughts. The desire was overwhelming: he decided he would take a few steps down the street all the same until he found a taxi, even though the consular instructions were never to walk alone after nightfall.

Aurel hadn't gone a hundred yards before voices revived him.

"Hey, White Guy, where you going?"

"Give me your money, *toubab*."

"Take care, sir, it's dangerous around here. Can I help you?"

Shadows coming out of the walls, following him, two boys pulling on his sleeves. As soon you left Le Cercle behind, there were no more streetlamps. Aurel walked faster. Oddly, he wasn't thinking about himself, but about Mayères. He imagined him alone on his boat in the dark of night, with all that money in his safe. Why had he chosen such a lifestyle? Why take such a huge risk? And what had he been looking for, exactly, through the narrow slit in his nav station?

Suddenly, a group of menacing figures gathered some distance ahead of him, in the halo of a streetlight. The group was watching Aurel as he trotted along, followed by the retinue of beggars he had in tow. As he got closer, he could see more clearly who made up the gang. They were young Africans wearing sleeveless jerseys and baseball caps. Fear suddenly banished any other thoughts Aurel might have. He thought he saw the flash of a blade. He'd been in a similar situation one evening long ago, when he was working in bars in Montmartre and was walking home, in the direction of the Porte de Saint-Ouen. He'd given them all the money he had, but since his aggressors didn't think it was enough, they'd smashed two of his teeth. Aurel put his hand in his pocket and felt for his wallet. He remembered he'd forgotten to go to the bank and had almost no cash. Automatically he looked behind him. Le Cercle was already far away. Some headlights were coming toward him. He stopped, hoping to see the little yellow shining light that indicated a taxi. But it was a private car. It would certainly drive by as fast as possible, as the consulate recommended foreign residents do at night. Aurel turned back toward the group of thugs. They were heading his way, walking abreast, leaving him no way to escape to the side. Catholics have a saint they turn to in desperate situations. Aurel invested all his energy in trying to remember his name. It helped him avoid thinking about the teeth he was about to lose.

But just then, as it drew level with him, the car slowed down and stopped. The window was rolled down, and a man's voice barked in French, "Get in, quick!"

Aurel opened the door and clambered into the car. At the very same moment, two of the hooligans, the quickest ones, leapt forward to grab him. The driver activated the safety device to lock the doors. There was a banging sound on the roof of the car. The attackers were hitting it with their palms of their hands. The car pulled away, and the gang drew back, so as not to get run over.

"It's you!" cried Aurel, on seeing the driver.

It was Cortegiani, hunched over the steering wheel; he was looking straight ahead.

"Thank you. If it weren't for you, I don't know what they would have done to me."

Cortegiani shrugged.

"What a tomfool idea to walk home."

"I thought I'd find a taxi . . ."

"You're lucky I got lost."

"You got lost?"

"All these damned little streets with no light . . . Just now when I left, I got in the car, which I'd parked outside Le Cercle, and headed off in the wrong direction. In the end I had to turn back and go all the way around."

"Lucky for me!"

"Right, where should I drop you off? I'm going back to the embassy."

"That's perfect: I live next door."

They turned onto a major road. Cortegiani was driving slowly, making a huge effort to concentrate. He held his liquor well, apparently, but his reflexes were nevertheless severely diminished, and there were times when he seemed confused. Aurel was afraid he might fall asleep. He kept talking to him to keep him awake. But a serious conversation was out of the question: Aurel limited himself to simple statements.

"The white wine at Le Cercle's not great, what do you think?"

"As far as I'm concerned, there's only whisky."

"I hear you," said Aurel, who couldn't stand the stuff.

At least he'd found a topic where Cortegiani seemed never to lack for words, and was even garrulous. The customs officer began enumerating the names of single malts Aurel had never heard of in his life. Their Celtic sonority roared from his mouth and blended marvelously with his thick elocution.

When they reached the center of town, just as they were going around a traffic circle, a trailer truck nearly ran into them. The fright brought the driver's Scottish inspiration to an abrupt end. They went the rest of the way in silence.

Back at his place, Aurel took an aspirin right away. His adventures on the way home had worn off some of the alcohol, but his overindulgence had left him with a stubborn headache.

He got undressed and put on his embroidered slippers and a sort of mohair dressing gown. He went into the kitchen and took half a chicken and some mustard from the fridge. Then, once he'd eaten, he got out a bottle of chilled white wine. Enough of that cheap wine from Le Cercle; no more thoughts of plonk, sparkling wine, or Anglo-Saxon rotgut. He was getting back to the fundamentals.

IX

For a full hour, he sat at the piano and played Mozart. His classical training left something to be desired, and he certainly didn't have the level of a concert pianist. Mozart, though, was sort of a last resort, a cure-all that calmed his anxiety, removed the ugliness of the everyday from his soul, and allowed him to enter the pure world of ideas. By the time he closed the keyboard, Aurel felt perfectly lucid and ready for the task at hand.

Now that he had so much information about Mayères, the time had come to put all the pieces together, at a distance from the day's upheavals. Aurel opened his computer, and while it was booting up, he went to take a box of thumbtacks from a drawer. Then he plugged in the printer and again copied out the victim's photo, this time in color. He pinned it at eye level on the wall in the living room, took a few steps back to consider the effect, then drew the outline of a body with a felt-tipped pen under the portrait. Now he was face-to-face with a life-size Mayères and could speak to him as an equal.

Next, he went to get the documents he'd found in the safe on the boat. To start with, there was a little plastic sleeve containing photographs. There were no captions, and they featured portraits and groups of people Aurel couldn't identify. In the safe, he'd also found a bunch of handwritten letters. There were two sets, bound together in separate packets.

The first consisted of around a dozen pages. He unfolded one. It was dated February 11, 2012. Aurel had some difficulty deciphering it. The handwriting was nervous and elliptical, the letters poorly formed. The text began, "My darling." He had to read several paragraphs and turn the pages over to find the signature before he understood. This letter, and the other ones in the packet, had been written by Mayères himself. To whom were they addressed? As he deciphered the contents of the letters, which were always fairly short but densely written, the words crammed together with little space between the lines, Aurel gradually understood. These weren't letters from a man in love, or rather, if they were about love, it wasn't in the context of a sexual relationship between a man and woman. It was above all about suffering, guilt, the future, childhood. Suddenly, one sentence illuminated everything: "Your mother and I were very hurt that you went through all that without calling us." Your mother and I: the letters were written to their daughter. From one of the headings, Aurel saw that her name was Cléo. Every page was steeped in regret and questioning about mistakes that had been made. Mayères admitted he'd spent too much time at work and had not been there for his daughter as he should have during her childhood. Everything else in the letters focused on money matters. It emerged that they had broken off their relations: the only tie that remained between Cléo and her father was her constant financial neediness. It also became clear that this money had fed her ever-increasing drug use. Mayères responded with love, sending the amounts she asked for. But in doing this, his love became a lethal instrument. The letters referred to accidents, assaults, and bouts in the hospital that were like so many painful stations along the young addict's way of the cross. Then came the begging, almost incoherent last letter, which must have been written in tears, illegible at the end. "Answer, please, answer me. I was wrong to refuse what you asked for. Tell me where I can come see you. Answer me, Cléo. Please don't keep silent. I love you more than you can know."

Aurel wiped his eyes. Then he looked at Mayères. There was a new expression on his face. The hardness of his features was, in fact, a sort of erosion, due to sorrow, to nights of anguish, to waiting for the news he expected or dreaded.

The letters Aurel held in his hand had probably been returned to sender after Cléo's death. The last one seemed to imply that her father, in desperation, must have changed tack and hardened his attitude, refusing to give her the money she asked for. God alone knew what the young woman went and did next. In any case, it killed her, and the guilt Mayères felt must have been devastating.

Aurel went back to the photographs. One of them showed a little girl, probably about eight years old, wearing a red smocked dress with a flowered collar. She had straight hair and dark, slightly asymmetrical eyes. Her smile was rigid, forced, almost painful. Aurel imagined the intense nostalgia her father must have felt in looking at this image from an earlier time. It would have taken him back to the days when everything was still possible, when the seed of misfortune and death had not yet sprouted. He tried to find a picture of the adult Cléo among the other photographs. He could only guess he'd found her in one shot that showed the family sitting in the sun around a table on a terrace. Aurel recognized Aimée among the women. An unfamiliar couple were sitting opposite her and, at the end of the table, hidden under a baseball cap, her eyes behind dark glasses, a very thin girl was holding a cigarette in one hand and a glass in the other. It was probably Cléo, come to see her parents for money, as always. There was a silent tension in the scene. Despite the sunshine, the bottles of wine, the Provençal dinnerware, the whole tableau had something funereal about it. Aurel wondered if this wasn't the last picture Mayères had of his daughter. He went up to the wall where he'd pinned the portrait and placed the two photographs on its right.

There were far fewer letters in the second batch. They were written very legibly, in turquoise ink. Aurel didn't need to be a handwriting expert to recognize a woman's hand right away. There was something admirable and terrifying about the regularity of the writing. It was as if the person with the pen in her hand made her way through life the way she did along the lines of the paper, without ever being sidetracked by anything, putting her plan into action, sticking to her habits, her methods, never letting anything alter those plans or diminish her confidence.

The letters were signed "A," and Aurel had no doubt in his mind: this meant Aimée.

They were cold, soulless letters, devoid of tenderness. But they were permeated with the sort of respect that might exist between two parties to a contract. In the most recent letter, Aimée wrote: "I have taken note of the plan you unveiled to me. I have no objections. You alone can be the judge of the direction you now intend to take in life. I'm sincerely happy that we have been able to come to an agreement, and I thank you for it."

This formula of gratitude—dry, with no other explanation—was the only concession Aimée seemed prepared to make to her feelings. What was she referring to? What was this agreement that she and Mayères had come to? The letter had been written not long before the sailboat left France for good. Aurel hunted for another picture of Aimée, didn't find any, so he digitized the one where she was featured with her daughter. By reframing the shot on the computer, he was able to print out an image of Aimée that was almost a close-up. He pinned it on the wall next to Mayères.

Another picture showed the victim together with some men and women who must have been his employees. Behind them was the entrance to a modern building, in all likelihood the company headquarters. Aurel stuck it on the wall. The last two photographs, with figured edges, were in black and white. One of them showed a soldier, full length, in uniform and with his weapons, probably the kind of portrait of a combatant that used to be taken before every war. On the last one, the same soldier, without his kepi and with his tunic unbuttoned, was holding a boy, ten years old or so, by the hand: this must have been Jacques Mayères with his older brother Robert, the hero. The boy was puffed up with pride, his nostrils flared, his eyes shining. He seemed to be electrified by the big hand he was squeezing in his little fingers, and it was easy to imagine how disappointed he would feel once that hand had let him go, his solitude. All the more so when he learned that he would never be able to hold it again, that it was buried lifeless in the ground, with neither volition nor memory. Aurel put the photograph on the wall. Now there were pictures all around Mayères. On the internet, he found one of Mame Fatim, published by a local newspaper. He printed it out and stuck it on the wall with the others.

Then he stepped back. Mayères was adrift in his world, with these satellites turning around him. They exerted their conflicting influences over the dead man. At first glance, it looked as if their forces were grouped in opposing pairs. The brother and the company. Aurel drew a line between the two images with a heavy black felt-tipped pen. On one side heroism, on the other, business. The mother's family, and the father's. Aimée and her daughter, another line: an ambivalent, deadly pair, consisting of a domineering mother and a child in love with her father. Aimée and Mame Fatim, another line, another opposition. The daughter and the company, an apparently ambiguous couple, the disappearances of one causing the sale of the other. Aurel found quite a few more lines to draw. They all went through Mayères's picture, and he now looked like a big bumblebee caught in a spider's web.

It was all inextricable. It was a life, and to varying degrees, every life has interlacing relationships, oppositions, contradictions. And yet, at some point, one of them had prevailed over the others and sliced through the Gordian knot. A shot had been fired, and everything had unraveled. But who had held the gun?

Aurel went over to the piano and played a Chopin sonata, very slowly, almost chord by chord. Suddenly he stood up, looked for something on his computer, found an image of the *Tlemcen*, printed it out and put it on the wall next to Mayères.

"This is the first break."

Mayères had broken every thread to set off on his boat.

Aurel sat down on the side of an armchair to give it some thought. Maybe he was headed down the wrong path, restoring all these memories and events to the space around Mayères? After all, Mayères had come to Conakry to leave them all behind. The entire case consisted of nothing more than a sailboat in a marina and a man without a past confronted with people who, all of a sudden, had surrounded and threatened him.

It was two o'clock in the morning when Aurel headed off in a new direction. He'd thought a great deal about this man who'd been bound by his past, and now he was finding out what he was like as a free man. Why burden him with everything he'd wanted to escape from? Wasn't the solution to be found by wiping the slate clean instead? A port in Africa, boats, a man and his fortune.

Aurel took down the photograph of the sailboat and put it to one side of the other prints. In the spider's web he had woven around Mayères, only Mame Fatim was local. He took down her photograph and put it next to the sailboat. He drew a figure on a sheet of paper, added it, and wrote "Lamine." Who else?

To stay lucid, Aurel had been careful not to drink too much. But having reached this point, obliged to rethink everything, he thought it was time for a little glass. He went and got a bottle of white, rinsed out a glass, and slowly drank the slightly maderized Chablis he'd found in his predecessor's cellar.

Since his reasoning had brought him back to boats, he went to the computer to look up the list Hassan had obtained for him.

It was a fairly long Excel spreadsheet, listing the name and flag of all the boats registered at the marina over the last six months, including the identity and nationality of their crew, their port of origin and destination, and finally their date of entry and departure from Guinean territorial waters.

As he hurried through the list, Aurel noticed for a start that there weren't that many sailing yachts. He could discern three types of sailing visitor: first, those who made a quick stopover and left again almost at once. Typically, boats like that were simply sailing along the coast of Africa. They made short passages that required little preparation. Next, there were those who stayed longer, a few days to a few weeks. Most of them were headed for Brazil. Conakry was their last African port of call. They had fairly long and exhaustive preparations to make for a crossing on the open ocean that would take several days. Finally, there were those, not that many, who settled in for several months, as Mayères had. Aurel noticed, while looking at the crews' characteristics, that this last option was adopted mainly by retired people or, on the other end of the spectrum, by couples with small children, often from Scandinavia or the Netherlands. In all likelihood these were families who, having opted for this vagabonding way of life, were taking their time, and staying in Conakry because they felt comfortable there.

Most of the boats on the list were foreign. A lot of Brits and Germans, a few Italians, and then the Dutch and Scandinavians. French boats were fairly rare. Aurel spent more time studying the end of the list: the last four boats registered were those still moored in the marina, and, consequently, they'd been present when the crime took place. Two of them were British. They had arrived from the same place, Dakar. The crews were couples in their seventies. They were obviously sailing together, because they'd arrived on the same day one month earlier. The commissaire had confirmed that both couples were on a trip to a nature reserve forty miles from Conakry on the night of the crime. Their presence had been vouched for at a hotel located at the edge of the reserve. The third boat was flying the Maltese flag. On board were a couple in their thirties with two children, aged five and seven. The man was American and his wife Australian. They had arrived shortly before Mayères. Often, this sort of family enrolled their children at the school in town and stayed for an entire school year. This was probably the case with this family since they'd arrived at the end of August, just before the children were due back at school. At first glance, there was no apparent reason to suspect them. Moreover, it looked as if Mayères had taken fright only lately, and this couple and their children had been his neighbors from the beginning and were not known to have bothered him in any way. The last sailboat belonged to a solo skipper: an Italian in his forties. Aurel had seen him on his boat, from a distance. A good-looking man, who went around bare-chested, proudly showing off all the tattoos on his shoulders. According to the list, his last port of call before arriving two weeks ago had been Lanzarote. His profile was suspicious for several reasons. Supposing the whole business had been masterminded by Aimée, this native of Genoa might provide the missing link. There was a good chance he spent a fair amount of time on the Riviera, where she might have met him. Moreover, the nature of his resources was unknown. Where had he got the money for such a magnificent schooner? It was perfectly feasible that he had links to the mafia and was involved in trafficking. And yet, he had an alibi that was both ridiculous and pretty solid:

he'd spent that night with the daughter of the public health minister. He'd been in the minister's very apartment; the minister himself was away on an official trip to China. Bâ had alluded to the event when Aurel met him in Dupertuis's office. Since then, a tabloid had reported on the affair and published the testimonies of several household staff members who confirmed the sailor's alibi. Aurel felt inclined to accept this version and didn't really believe such a character could be implicated in Mayères's murder: as far as he was concerned, this particular Italian was almost too suspicious to be guilty. However, he couldn't rule anything out. Aurel outlined a figure on a sheet of paper and wrote Gian-Carlo. Then he put it on the wall next to the sailboat, alongside Mame Fatim and Lamine.

He looked at his list again and this time went higher up, skipping over the previous months. If it was true that the marina was a hub for drug trafficking, there were bound to be a few crews that were involved. But, with the exception of one or two fishy characters like Gian-Carlo, they all seemed irreproachable. Which begged a very simple question, one Aurel had never asked: who exactly is it that gets involved in this sort of trafficking? If he put himself in the shoes of the traffickers for a moment, it became obvious that they would prefer to use people who, at first glance, appeared above suspicion. Aurel recalled having read an article somewhere about an elderly couple, almost in their eighties, who used their RV to smuggle cocaine . . .

Viewed from this angle, the world changed its appearance, and an abyss opened at your feet. Those fine sailboats bobbing in the sun on the waters of the marina, with their easy-going, good-natured crews: they suddenly wore the terrifying mask of the mafia and the drug world. When he lived in Romania, Aurel had grown accustomed to this permanent union of respectability and crime. Communist dignitaries had all worn a veneer of undying allegiance to Marxism, as if butter wouldn't melt in their mouths. And yet beneath their masks they hid corruption, mendacity, and violence. When he arrived in the West, Aurel wanted to believe that he'd reached a land of truth where all the bad guys looked like bad guys, and where the good guys could be trusted. Deep down, he knew this couldn't be true. But he wanted to believe it. Mayères, on the other hand, had probably never believed it.

Out of curiosity, Aurel typed on his keyboard to find out when the last major drug seizure had taken place in the area. The only case recorded on the internet was the interception of a sailboat by a French escort vessel in international waters off the Ivory Coast. The incident had occurred four months earlier. Further searching gave Aurel the name of the boat: the *Cork*. On board were two women in their sixties, widows, Irish nationals. One of them was a former math teacher and the other a nurse. They had taken up cruising for pleasure several months before. Aurel then referred to the list from the harbor master. Going back to the period in question, he found the *Cork*. The two women had arrived on a Tuesday and left the following Sunday. Their identity was given on the spreadsheet. How might they have been found out? So that was it, then: no one was above suspicion. These dignified retired couples, these holy families, these golden boys who had worked for this life of sunshine and *far niente*: all of them, absolutely every last one, were potential smugglers. No one could be ruled out.

Aurel took a sheet of paper and drew the little Australo-American family on it. Figuring that he had eliminated the family from his list of suspects a bit too hastily, he pinned them to the wall. After thinking for a moment, he added another sheet with the names of the four Brits. Everyone, in this enclosed little world, was suspicious. And so was Mayères.

Aurel had reasoned, rather hastily, that Mayères's money exempted him from having to play this sort of game. But what did he know, in the end? Who could guarantee that he, too, was not involved in trafficking? Who could swear he didn't have dangerous acquaintances? Aurel printed out Mayères's picture once again and put it next to the sailboat. He stood back and considered the effect. On the wall he had reconstituted an almost complete picture of the marina. Only Seydou and the boss were missing. He added them, then played at rearranging the clusters of papers on the wall, so that they would be where all the protagonists actually were. He placed all the sailboats in one corner, and Mayères's on its own, at the other end of the marina. He drew the clubhouse in its place on the wall and pinned the boss's picture alongside. He put Seydou on the shore and posted the effigies of Mame Fatim and Lamine in between Seydou and Mayères's boat. Then, pleased with his work, he poured another drink.

He now had two ensembles on the wall: Mayères in the spider's web of his family, and Mayères in the middle of the marina. He tugged on the sofa and swung it around to bring it closer to the wall, directly opposite the two diagrams, then he slumped onto it. For Aurel, reflection often led to drowsiness. Many of his bosses and torturers had been misled by this. They thought he was asleep, but in fact he was indulging in interesting ruminations, and they were always surprised by what he came out with.

Time passed. Now and again Aurel opened an eye, reached out his arm for a bit more white wine, drank, then collapsed again on the cushions, his eyes half-closed. At one point, he fell asleep for good, then woke with a start. He was frightened. What, Aurel frightened? No, he thought, as he regained his wits, it's Mayères who's frightened. And this, only recently. Frightened of whom? This dreamlike method enabled him to identify fully with his protagonist. He loved this role-playing; he eventually managed to see the world through the eyes of those whose place he'd happily taken. Through the dead man's

eyes, he could see Aimée, Cléo, the warp and weft of his former life: he didn't feel any danger coming from that direction.
The terror was coming from the marina. But from whom?
Several times he reimmersed himself in his dreams and
emerged with a sudden start, staring at the map of the little
harbor. Every time, the fear was there. He could feel it vibrat-
ing inside him like a pendulum. But the fear didn't focus on
anyone.

Time was passing. The night had begun to take on a rosy
hue. There were more and more spots of light breaking
through the barrier of vegetation over his windows.

Suddenly, Aurel sat up and let out a shout. He saw it. He
saw *what was missing*. The most important thing, and it had
nothing to do with the papers he'd stuck on the wall, but with
the hole that, all together, they surrounded.

Now that he'd got it, the entire mechanism clicked into
place, and started working properly, thanks to this missing
piece. Mayères's past, everything he'd done since arriving in
Conakry, the various testimonies people had given: everything
reshuffled. Through a sort of miracle, where before there had
been only incoherence and mystery, there was now harmony,
logic, and truth. Aurel was on his feet, rubbing his hand over
his face.

He stood like that for a long while, stunned, the first to be
surprised by the simplicity of his deductions. He felt like someone who has just recovered from a raging fever. He very nearly
decided to rush out there and then, so clear was it to him what
he had to do. But suddenly, like Adam called by his Maker, he
became aware of his nakedness. He hurried to his wardrobe
and took out literally anything his hand alighted on. Some old
corduroy trousers he ordinarily kept for Sunday strolls on the
golf course. A blue turtleneck sweater and, over that, a dinner
jacket. Without thinking, he put on a tie over his turtleneck.
Then he dug around at the bottom of the wardrobe for a pair

158 · JEAN-CHRISTOPHE RUFIN

of shoes. He took the first ones he found, burgundy loafers with tassels, and put them on, not bothering with socks. He grabbed his wallet and keys from a table by the door and went out into the little street.

One of his neighbors two doors down was a taxi driver: Aurel found him out front washing his car. He went up to him and, not saying a word, climbed in the back of the car. The man had no intention of starting work this early, and he hadn't finished rinsing off his old Renault. But he knew Aurel and was well aware that it was hard to argue with him. He left his bucket by the door and climbed into the car, which was still dripping with foam. His hands were sopping wet, so he held the wheel with his wrists.

"To the marina," trumpeted Aurel.

X

At dawn, the city was teeming with pedestrians: according to a universal law, to which Conakry is no exception, poor people have to get up earlier than everyone else. Hordes of men and women were moving along, carrying bundles or plastic basins on their heads. Among them were schoolchildren in bright uniforms and office employees in Western suits, their shoes covered in dust but their white shirts immaculate. The heat had already arrived, but it circled on itself like a bird of prey.

For a while yet, the crowd would make its way through the cool shade that had not completely disappeared. Down this street or that, the sun appeared fleetingly between two buildings, painting them a reddish gold. In less than an hour, everything would be glare and dust, but for the moment, the struggle was almost equal between the moist breath of night and the parched incandescence of early morning.

The gate to the marina was shut every evening. It was a useless precaution: the wall that was meant to enclose the garden had collapsed in a number of places, offering multiple ways to get into the facility. Moreover, the gate had merely been pushed to, and Aurel had no problem getting in. He walked on, passing the clubhouse building on his left, its windows covered by wooden shutters. The boss was still sleeping. He never got up before nine or ten o'clock. Aurel headed toward the marina, and, on his right, at the far end of the garden, he saw Seydou's hut.

160 · JEAN-CHRISTOPHE RUFIN

The young man was already up. A tin saucepan was heating on two stones. Leaning over the smoking wood fire, he was slowly waking up. When he saw Aurel, he wiped his hand over his eyes, as if to make sure he wasn't dreaming. As soon as he realized the consul was headed his way, he took fright and sat up. Seydou had only had to deal with Hassan until now. He'd seen Aurel from a distance the day of his first visit—the day of the crime—and he'd taken him out to the sailboat with Jocelyne. He was aware of his reputation and knew that all the whites made fun of him. But still, his appearance in the early morning was enough to spook him. There was his get-up, for one thing, which made him look completely crazy. But it was above all his haunted expression that struck terror into a young man like Seydou, for whom spirits and their ability to steal the souls of the living were an indisputable reality.

"You're Seydou, right?"

"Yes."

"I have a few questions for you."

As with Hassan, the boy's youth led Aurel instinctively to say *tu* to him.

"Would you like to sit down?" said Seydou hastily, pointing to a wobbly wooden stool. "I was just making some coffee . . ."

In African culture, there is nothing more unseemly than to go straight to the matter at hand. Traditions of hospitality require hosts to put their guests at ease. And the guests must take their time before getting to the purpose of their visit. But Aurel was well beyond all such considerations. The alcohol hadn't quite worn off, and he was still reeling from the dreamlike revelations he'd just experienced. In a world like that, you don't sit down, and you don't make polite small talk.

"You said you rowed Mame Fatim ashore that evening, when she left the sailboat to go and see her boyfriend Lamine."

"Yes," said Seydou.

He was sorry he'd opened up to Hassan. Aurel would go and tell everyone, and the boss was bound to find out.

"As a rule, you took her ashore. Did you also row her out to the sailboat when she came back?"

Seydou thought for a moment, not to find the answer— that, he knew—but to try and imagine which confession would be the least serious, if it were to become more widely known.

"To be honest, it varied from one time to the next. If she didn't get back too late, she would ask me. Otherwise, it was Lamine who brought her back."

"Was it always your boat?"

"What do you mean?"

"I mean, if you were sleeping, did they still take your boat?"

"Generally. But if I'd gone somewhere with it, they could use another one. You saw that there are plenty tied up along the shore."

"This one here, it's your boat?"

Aurel pointed to the little skiff tied up by the hut.

"You know it is. You've been in it yourself."

"And it has to be rowed?" Aurel insisted, sticking to his theory.

Seydou shrugged, it was such an obvious question.

"With one oar?"

"Why are you asking me all this: you can see it there, the oar."

"And you don't have another oar in the boat?"

"Don't you see how small it is? Where would I have room for another oar? And for what?"

Aurel didn't listen to his answer. He was on a scent, like a hunting dog. And he'd just found a first clue: he was on the right track. He looked up.

"Mame Fatim came back on board the *Tlemcen* in a boat with *two* oars."

"How do you know?"

"The music, my boy, the music," said Aurel, patting the young man on the shoulder. "I hear it, don't you know? I hear it like Teresa Berganza in Cherubino's aria in *Le Nozze di Figaro.*"

He hummed a few notes, drawing arabesques in the air. Then, suddenly, he changed register and imitated Mame Fatim's voice.

"Lamine put one of the two oars inside the dinghy and used the other to move forward slowly . . ."

"She said that?"

"Of course she did! *She's* the one who just spoke."

And Aurel again imitated the young woman, simpering and breathing in Seydou's face. The smell of alcohol on his breath made Seydou recoil.

"So that means they took another boat," the young man concluded.

"Exactly. And yet, yours had been moved. Are you sure?"

"Positive. I always tie it up the same way, backwards, so to speak, so that it's ready to go."

"And that time it was forwards."

"Yes."

"Which means that whoever put it back didn't know that you parked it like that."

"Probably not."

"Or else," Aurel added, increasingly perky, his finger in the air, "it meant they were in a hurry, whoever it was, and they didn't have time to waste on maneuvers."

Seydou thought to himself that this poor consul really was a little deranged. He felt like laughing, seeing him in that get-up of his, going into all this fuss about a boat. He went back to his little fire, took the lid off the saucepan, and poured some coffee into a thick glass.

"Are you sure you don't want any?"

Aurel turned around and seemed to see the hut with the little hearth burning in front of it for the first time.

"Oh, yes," he said, coming closer, "that's a good idea. A nice hot coffee."

And noticing a stool, he sat down, pulling up his corduroy trouser legs.

"Sugar?"

"Never, thank you."

Aurel took the glass Seydou handed him and stared at the black surface of the coffee, which was gleaming with oily patches.

"Something else now. You told Hassan that you had helped with another sailboat. A boat you said left the marina at the end of the afternoon before the night of the crime."

This was the missing piece, the hole in the diagram on the wall . . .

"I'd like you to tell me a little about that sailboat."

"If you like."

"What time exactly did it leave?"

"I'd say at five o'clock. Just before nightfall, in any case."

"And was Mayères on deck on his sailboat just then?"

"Yes, I saw him."

"And was he alive?"

"Don't make fun of me, Monsieur le Consul."

"I mean, was he moving? Did he wave to the boat that was leaving? Apparently that's what people do, especially in a small marina like this one."

"Mayères was moving, that's for sure; he was on deck, walking back and forth. I don't know if he waved."

"Where had this sailboat been moored?"

"Over there."

Seydou pointed toward the spot where the other sailboats were clustered.

"With the others, more or less?"

"Not really. It was between them and Monsieur Mayères's. It was actually kind of strange."

"And how long had it been there?"

"Two days."

"So it was registered with your boss, but not yet on the Maritime Affairs list."

"I don't really know, but probably not. The boss goes there once or twice a month, to give them the forms."

"And how many people were there in the crew?"

"Two: a man and a woman. South Africans."

"White?"

"As white as they come, yes."

"How old?"

"In their forties."

"Where were they going?"

"Home. They were headed for Durban, stopping off along the coast."

"Had you already seen them?"

"On their outbound trip, they stopped here."

"How long ago?"

"I don't know exactly. A few months."

"And what was the name of the boat?"

"The *Good Hope*."

Aurel took in the name along with a big swallow of coffee, which was beginning to cool down. He made a face.

"How strange. Don't you prefer tea? Guineans generally like tea."

"The boss gives me coffee," Seydou confessed, somewhat ill at ease.

That skinflint Ravigot clearly didn't give him top quality.

"Now, let's get down to the details, Seydou. I have two or three more questions; after that, I'll leave you alone. You said you went back and forth between the sailboats and the shore a few times on the day of the crime. Who did you take?"

"First of all the Brits, who were going on a photo safari. I dropped all four of them off, two at a time; I can't take more than that in my skiff. Then I did another trip for their luggage. That was at the beginning of the afternoon."

"And then?"

"And then I took one of the kids from the American family. He had to go to the doctor with his mother. I took them ashore and brought them back in the evening, when they came back."

"And nothing for the *Good Hope*?"

"Yes, in between the other two. They waved to me. I went over to see them. The guy didn't speak very good French, but he got me to understand that his rubber dinghy wasn't available. You know what they're like, these yachting people: as a rule, they go everywhere on the outboard. They don't know how to row."

"Why did they need their dinghy?"

"To load their provisions, which had been delivered and were waiting at the clubhouse."

"Was that all?"

"No, they wanted me to take a friend of theirs into town."

"A friend who was on board with them?"

"Yes."

"When and how did he arrive?"

"They didn't give me the details. And anyway, like I already said, they didn't speak much French."

"But you have an idea? How had he gotten on board, that friend of theirs?"

Aurel was taking little sips of his coffee. The bitterness of the watery brew was far more efficient in waking him up than any amount of caffeine it might contain.

"How should I know? Maybe their outboard was working earlier and they went to get him themselves."

"But you didn't see them do that?"

"I'm not always down here by the water. At mealtimes, I help the boss at the clubhouse."

"But maybe he actually came with them on the sailboat?"

"That could be, too. I have no idea."

"And what was he like, this friend? Was he South African, too?"

"He might've been, but that would surprise me. He looked more like an Indian, not an Indian from India, an Indian like in a Western, you know what I mean?"

"Tall?"

"Not very, but well-built. Broad shoulders, like this, and muscles showing through his shirt . . ."

"So, you took him ashore, and they stayed on board, is that it?"

"Yes."

"Did he have any luggage?"

"A little backpack, not much in it."

"And where was he going?"

"How should I know? I dropped him off, and he walked toward the gate."

The coffee was finished, the conversation, too. Aurel stood up and tugged on his jacket.

"Thank you, Seydou."

"Please, Monsieur le Consul, I told you all this, but if the boss . . ."

The young man glanced anxiously toward the clubhouse, where the shutters, thankfully, were still closed.

"Fear not. I shall put all this to excellent use, and Ravigot will be none the wiser."

After this assurance proclaimed in a manner worthy of the best seventeenth-century orators, Aurel went back to the exit, grimacing: his fine loafers were once again full of sand.

* * *

The taxi driver dropped Aurel off outside the embassy, where his get-up and his demeanor had quite an effect on the gendarmes. To avoid their ironical stares, he put on his glacier glasses, which didn't help matters.

He found a note on his desk, which Lemenêtrier had left there the day before. It read:

"The consul general will be coming home tonight. There will be a staff meeting tomorrow morning. If you cannot attend, please provide me with a short summary regarding the Mayères affair, since you've been following it."

Aurel crumpled the paper and tossed it in the waste basket. Then he turned on his computer. Mayères's portrait appeared on the desktop. Aurel gazed at it for a long while: "You really had me there," he murmured. "You're really good at hiding your game. I can see why they turned to you. But don't worry. Justice will be served. And soon."

Then he clicked on a file, and the list of boats that had passed through the marina appeared on the screen. To Aurel, this was a mere formality. When there is this much cross-checking, intuition becomes certainty. All the same, his heart gave a little flutter when he saw the name of the *Good Hope* show up exactly where he'd expected it to. Four months earlier, at the same time as the *Cork* and its cargo of drugs, and just before the French had inspected the *Cork* on the high seas.

He checked the time: half past eight. He figured it would be all right to call Jocelyne now. She was having breakfast out on the terrace of her hotel.

"Your voice sounds strange, Aurel. Did you sleep all right?"

"That's why I'm calling. Here's what I have to tell you: I didn't sleep *a wink*. But I put the time to good use. I think it's in the bag."

"What do you mean?"

"I've tied up just about all the threads."

"Good for you! Tell me!"

"I can't. Certainly not over the phone. Just one thing you

should know. To get at the murderers, we're going to have to . . . blow the system wide open."

"Be more explicit. I absolutely do not understand what you mean."

"It doesn't matter. Do you still trust me?"

"More than ever."

"Well then, be ready to help me this evening. Ready for whatever it takes."

"My goodness, that's a bit much!"

Aurel was troubled when he remembered who he was talking to.

"It's not that."

"What do you mean by 'that?'"

Aurel was as embarrassed as could be.

"Please stop," he moaned. "I'm serious."

"Forgive me."

"Listen carefully: I'm going to try and get some sleep because I need to have my mind totally clear tonight. Between now and then, don't leave the hotel; you get some rest, too. Then come and meet me at my home at half past eight."

"Gladly, but where is it?"

"I'll send the car to pick you up. Above all, when you come into my house, give your first name only."

"What a mystery! Well, you can count on me. Sleep well."

She gave a clear laugh that ate at Aurel's heart. He pictured her, her hair held in a blue scarf, yes, blue, because it was the color that suited her best, in the shade of the parasol, her face lit by the sun glancing off the white tablecloth, there by the sea . . .

Mechanically, he clicked on the X to close the Maritime Affairs file, and Mayères's face reappeared, his eyes full of reproach.

"Forgive me," said Aurel, sincerely embarrassed.

And to make himself feel more at ease, he switched off the screen.

He had just one thing left to do before going home for some rest. There was a great deal at stake. His throat felt tight. To breathe easier, since he couldn't remove his turtleneck, he took off the tie he had knotted on top of it. Then he picked up the phone, and off he went.

"Hello, Cortegiani? Did you get back all right yesterday? Thank you again . . . I really owe you . . . If it hadn't been for you, those thugs . . . Well, I promised I would make it up to you . . . And now I've got the opportunity. I just received a gift from France. Some first-class whisky, as it happens . . . Thirty years. What do you say? . . . Right, I'll see you at my house tonight . . ."

There was a pause while his interlocutor went to check his schedule. Aurel would have given anything for a glass of water. The pause was taking a while. He rolled a cigarette back and forth between his fingers, and all of a sudden, the pale tobacco burst through the torn paper into his hand. He felt as if he were about to collapse on his desk from fatigue. Finally there was a sound on the other end of the line.

"Okay," said Cortegiani.

"Terrific! You have my address. It's where you dropped me off. Fine . . . I'll expect you at around seven o'clock."

His voice had broken on saying these last words, but Cortegiani repeated them exactly, seven o'clock.

It was all set up.

* * *

By the time he finished a few things at the office, went home, and found some peace and quiet, Aurel didn't get to sleep before eleven A.M. He'd put an alarm clock next to his bed, to be on the safe side, but he didn't need it. At five minutes to five in the afternoon, he woke up spontaneously.

He had just over two hours to get ready. It was barely

enough. First of all, he had his own person to see to, like a toreador or a gladiator. He took a long shower, then shaved his scrawny beard, lathering his entire face with foam. He combed his hair and trimmed a few locks on the sides and behind, with the help of a little mirror. He filed his nails and anointed himself with a body lotion he'd taken from the hotel room in Italy during his last vacation, rubbing it into every inch of his skin. Then he readied the apartment. The biggest problem was the wall where he'd put up his two collages regarding Mayères. He would have liked to move them, but where to? He had to keep them readily accessible and, at the same time, make them invisible, at least to begin with. In the end, he went and took the bedspread from the spare room. It was made of a thick red damask fabric and resembled a theater curtain. On the wall, it would hide his display and give the room a particular charm, very central European, really. It looked out of place in this part of the world but would go well with Aurel's personality, particularly that evening. Then there was the piano. In the game that was about to be played, it was the showpiece. Aurel moved it around several times, and, sweating profusely, he eventually found the spot that suited him: practically in the middle of the room, with no obstacles to the right, or the left, or in front, which gave him great tactical freedom. Once he had finished these arrangements, Aurel sprayed himself with cologne. He felt like a gladiator about to enter the arena for a duel unto the death. What he was about to do was so unreasonable that it could be likened if not to a suicide attempt at least to deliberate self-destruction. At the same time, he had the prospect of some real entertainment and of carrying out an act of justice. Everything he liked in life, in other words.

He chose an appropriate outfit. It had to be dark (it was evening), fairly formal but not too much so (he was at home). Above all, it had to leave him free to move. He chose a pair of black flannel trousers he'd bought in Linz a few years earlier.

It had been not long after he separated from his wife, and he'd put on a lot of weight. It had taken less than a year for him to go back to his usual weight; the clothing he'd bought during that period brought up painful memories. He'd gotten rid of nearly everything except these trousers. They were much too warm for this climate, but he didn't care: they were loose, and they wouldn't hinder his movements, and that was the main thing. Initially, he decided not to wear a jacket. Then he picked out a dark blue double-breasted blazer that he would take off as soon as his guest arrived, to put him at ease. So he would be in his shirt for most of the evening. Jocelyne's presence incited him to choose the shirt carefully. He wanted to look his best for her. He eventually chose a white shirt with a jabot and puffy sleeves. It was practically a relic. He used to wear it back in the days when he was the pianist at a music hall on the Place Blanche. The act was called *The Little Women of Versailles*. The dancers wore costumes from the Ancien Régime. So that he would match, they had gratified him with this frilly shirt worthy of a seventeenth-century character like Sganarelle. Those were reasonably good memories. He used to think he was handsome, dressed like that, and he was briefly popular with the women. One of the girls in the troupe had even given him a rendezvous—who knows what might have happened if he'd been able to go? Unfortunately, the night before, as he was climbing back up the stairs to his maid's room on the eighth floor, he had a fall. He'd certainly had too much to drink. He had only himself to blame for breaking his arm. They kicked him out of the music hall, and all that remained of that happy interlude was this shirt. It had hardly yellowed at all. It was cut in a cloth of excellent quality. He slipped it on and looked at himself in the mirror. To be sure, he was no longer twenty years old, but the shirt still gave him an air that was sentimental and wanton at the same time, a throwback, in his opinion, to all the charms of the eighteenth century. His guests might find it rather strange. But he was used to disregarding convention and formulating his own decrees of what constituted elegance.

Once these issues had been dealt with, there were a few minor details left, although in this regard, as the Japanese had taught him, "every hair of the lion is a lion": the glasses, the whisky bottle, a bowl of pistachios, and two new candles on the piano.

At half past six, everything was ready. He poured himself a glass of nicely chilled Tokaji, sat down on the sofa in the living room, and waited, rehearsing his role.

* * *

He must have nodded off, because the doorbell caused him to leap up from the sofa. A quick glance around to make sure nothing was missing, and he went to open the door.

It was dark out, and the entrance was poorly lit. Cortegiani, his head hunched between his shoulders, greeted him with a grunt and came in. Aurel stood behind him and insisted on taking his jacket. Once he had hung it in the cupboard along with his own, he returned to his guest and found him studying the décor. The red tapestry, the candles on the piano, the bottle in front of the sofa with the two glasses: the customs man was visibly wondering what he was in for. When he saw Aurel in the light, he stared at him from head to foot. With his ruffled shirt, his lacquered hair, and the smell of perfume he gave off, the consul contrasted sharply with the shabbily dressed customs man who'd come straight from the office.

Cortegiani looked straight ahead, snorting noisily, like a bull about to charge. Aurel suddenly realized how a misunderstanding might arise. He had thought of a lot of things, of everything, or so it had seemed. But he hadn't foreseen this particular reaction.

"A lady friend will be joining us a bit later," he said precipitously, to remove any ambiguity.

Unfortunately, although this information did reassure the customs man on one account, it aroused another sort of wariness.

"A lady friend? And who might that be?"

Used to dealing with mafia types, Cortegiani was familiar, at least on paper, with all the tricks they could come up with to thwart agents whose job it was to restrain them. He wondered if he'd been wrong to confide in this Aurel person. An eccentric of this sort must fall into every trap and could, consciously or unwittingly, serve as an instrument to provocation.

"A French tourist, passing through," said Aurel. "Don't worry. A charming lady of utmost discretion."

Cortegiani shot him a suspicious look but relaxed. After all, he'd have plenty of time to make up his own mind when the creature appeared.

"Not a bad place you've got here."

"Thank you. Very kind of you to say so. I've picked up a few knickknacks over the years."

Cortegiani walked around the living room, pausing to look at the books and paintings.

"Do you like Klimt?" asked Aurel eagerly.

"Dunno much about all that. But it's pretty."

Pretty. If he hadn't known what he had in store, Aurel would have thrown the boor out. But he remained calm: *All sins will be counted. And punishment will fall on the wicked.*

"So, shall we get started on this whisky?" he exclaimed gaily, leading his visitor to the center of the room.

"With pleasure. Let's have a look. Ah! A thirty-year-old Edradour. I know this one. A good choice."

"What makes you so sure?"

"What do you mean," Cortegiani protested. "I told you, I know this one. It's the smallest distillery in Scotland.

Handmade. Actually, I don't know how you managed to get your hands on it."

"You may have already tasted Edradour, but you haven't tasted *mine*," said Aurel, adopting the Yiddish intonation of the old rabbi who used to live across the street when he was twelve years old.

He grabbed hold of the bottle and, still making cheerful faces, removed the stopper. He poured a generous amount in Cortegiani's glass and handed it to him.

"Thank you. What about you?"

"No, the whisky is for you. My doctor has recommended I stick to white wine."

He saw a shadow of suspicion darken his guest's gaze. Did he fear he was about to be poisoned? To overcome this last resistance, Aurel poured himself a splash of whisky.

"Just a drop, then, for the toast. But the rest, I promise, is for you. I'll go back to my white wine."

Once he was sure he'd gained Cortegiani's trust, Aurel would rely on his ability to entertain him and make him set aside his reservations. He'd worked as an entertainer for years, and he knew how to make his clients relax until they turned excited and giddy, without ever losing his own lucidity or his underlying melancholy. He summoned all his talent to strip Cortegiani of his stiff manner and make him lower his guard.

"So, what do you think of my whisky?"

"It's marvelous."

"You say that, but you've hardly had any! Here, let me pour you some more."

"Thank you, thank you!"

Then came the question Aurel had been waiting for.

"Do you play the piano?" asked Cortegiani.

Aurel had done well to put the instrument in the middle of the room. Who knew whether this oaf would have noticed it otherwise . . .

"I was a pianist in my younger days."

"Really? Concerts, all that sort of thing?"

"No," Aurel replied modestly, "more like café-concerts . . . Go on, ask me for a tune, any tune, some music you like."

"I have no idea. Wait . . ."

"Take your time."

Up to now, in their tête-à-tête, Cortegiani had not been in the habit of making Aurel wait endlessly for his replies. It had been possible to have a more or less normal conversation with him. But this question drove him straight back inside himself again—motionless, absent, elsewhere.

Aurel, who was hovering by the piano, was about to start making suggestions when, finally, Cortegiani solemnly declared: "'O Bella Ciao.'"

"'O Bella Ciao'?"

"Yes."

Cortegiani bowed his head, as if he had said something improper.

"Well, of course."

Aurel swung around on the piano stool and began to play. It took him a few seconds to get into it, but then there it was: the strains of "O Bella Ciao" filling the room.

"*Una mattina, mi son svegliato, o bella ciao, o bella ciao, o bella ciao ciao ciao . . .*"

Aurel's voice was deeper than his build might have suggested. His range was almost that of a baritone. But an agitated baritone, who bounced on his stool and stretched his neck when he reached for the high notes.

By the third verse, Cortegiani had joined in.

"*E se io muoio da partigiano,*" he bellowed, "*tu mi devi seppellir.*"

He clapped his hands like a little kid when the song was over.

"Something else?" asked Aurel, careful to refill the whisky glass.

"Do you know 'Georgia on My Mind'?"

"Do I know it? Just call me Ray Charles!"

Aurel went to get his glacier glasses, which he'd left on a console, then sat back down at the piano. He played leaning backwards and looking up.

Georgia, Georgia,
the whole day through
just an old sweet song
keeps Georgia on my mind.

Cortegiani had a bit more trouble with the English lyrics, but he bawled the refrain without restraint. Aurel performed a series of priceless mimes, as if he were expressing all the sorrow of the poor blind singer. He began improvising on the theme, transforming the tune, slowing down and singing in a deep hollow voice, or speeding up with a furious jazzy rhythm. Cortegiani was clapping his hands and laughing louder and louder. The level of whisky in the bottle was going down nicely. Fortunately Aurel had thought to have two more in reserve.

Suddenly the doorbell rang.

"Would you mind opening the door, please?"

Aurel was in the middle of an improvisation and didn't want to spoil the mood.

Cortegiani stood up and went to open the door. Jocelyne Mayères came in. She was wearing very flattering, well-cut black jeans. On her T-shirt, a scattering of little gold stars outlined the head of a cat.

Cortegiani would probably have felt flustered by her presence, but the considerable effect of the whisky, combined with the music-hall atmosphere, enabled him to greet her with a clumsy effort at a smile.

"Jocelyne," she said, holding out her hand.

"Norbert."

Well, thought Aurel, *I didn't even know his name*. And he immediately began to improvise to the tune of "Ring My Bell."

Norbert opened for the belle
Ring my bell
Ah, the belle.

"Well, I must say, Aurel, there's quite an atmosphere in here."

"We've only been waiting for you to start dancing, my friend. Help yourself to something to drink. And give Norbert a top-up, too, please. He's barely had anything to drink."

Jocelyne filled Cortegiani's glass and poured herself some white wine. She went over to Aurel, who was still pounding away on the piano, and she was about to fill his glass when he motioned to her not to. The quick look he gave her was so cool, so controlled, and in such contrast to the disorderly agitation he was pretending to indulge in that she paused briefly. With a quick thrust of his chin he indicated Cortegiani, who was holding his glass and gently tapping his foot in time. He looked a bit dazed, staring into space, his jowls drooping.

"Everything okay, Norbert?" shouted Aurel.

"Yes! But . . . Excuse me . . . Where can I . . . wash my hands?"

"End of the corridor on the right, same as everywhere."

Cortegiani stood up, staggered along the dark corridor, and disappeared behind the bathroom door. Playing all the while, Aurel motioned to Jocelyne to come closer and whispered in her ear.

"When he comes back, that's when we'll act. Do exactly as I tell you."

XI

Cortegiani came back and sat down. He must have splashed his face, and seemed slightly more alert. Jocelyne had filled his glass, and she insisted he empty it. Aurel redoubled his enthusiasm at the keyboard. He sang one of his own compositions: the music was a sort of Hungarian waltz, and the words made no sense whatsoever.

Cortegiani was slumped on the sofa. Jocelyne was sincerely beginning to wonder what she had got herself into. The time had come for action.

"Do you know how to play the piano, Cortegiani?" said Aurel.

"Huh, what, me?"

"Yes, the piano."

"No, no," said Cortegiani, waving him away, as if a street vendor were showing him some item he didn't want.

"I'm sure you could, though. It's really easy, look."

Aurel made his fingers dance along the bone keyboard, repeating a simple chord at different octaves.

"Sit down here next to me. I'll show you."

"No, no. I'm fine like this, thank you."

"Oh, do! Monsieur Cortegiani, please, go on," insisted Jocelyne, after Aurel had nodded to her.

Cortegiani found it more difficult to turn down a request from a woman. When Jocelyne took him by the arm, he no longer had the strength to resist. With a cackle, to show he wasn't taking any of this at all seriously, he stood up and went to sit on the big piano stool, well apart from Aurel, on his left.

"Well?"

"We're going to play 'Rock Around the Clock.' Do you know that one? You must have danced to it in your younger days."

Aurel played the melody very quickly with his right hand.

"Fine. Fine."

"So you'll play the bass. You're going to provide the rhythm."

He prepared the chord with his left hand, then struck it as if he were keeping time. Cortegiani shrugged.

"How do you want me to—"

"Put your hands on the keyboard. Both of them. Yes. And look, you place your fingers on these two white keys and this black one."

Cortegiani let Aurel spread his fingers for him.

"Try to strike the keys, keeping time."

Miracle: the bass notes from "Rock Around the Clock" burst forth from the piano.

"Go on. With the other hand, too. Yes! Yes!"

Against the background of bass notes, Aurel with his right hand made the melody dance. The combined result was more or less successful. Cortegiani was laughing like a kid.

"You see? You see? You're good at it, my man! Okay, let's start again."

Cortegiani was more convincing this time. He sat up straighter, placed his hands flat on the keys. Aurel glanced at Jocelyne, and there was such a chill to his gaze that she froze. Everything happened then in an instant.

Just as Cortegiani was expecting Aurel to begin playing again, Aurel leapt up. With one swift movement, he closed the lid to the keyboard, making it come down like a wooden guillotine on Cortegiani's hands, still spread along the keys. And with another leap, Aurel turned and sat with all his weight on the lid. Cortegiani screamed.

"But what—" said Jocelyne, tentatively.

"Just let me take care of this. Above all, don't move."

Aurel's face had changed. Leering demonically, his eyes bright with sobriety, he leaned over Cortegiani.

"Did he call you that last day?"

The pain was so extreme that Cortegiani briefly lost consciousness: with his hands still wedged in the piano, he was slipping forward. Aurel, merciless, bounced on his behind to increase the pressure of the wooden jaws and rouse Cortegiani.

"I asked you a question. Did Mayères call you the day he died?"

"Mayères?"

"Yes, Mayères."

"I . . . I . . . Let go . . . my hands . . . Aah! Please . . ."

As he emerged from his torpor, the pain returned, unbearable, and the cries he uttered were excruciating.

"Yes or no?"

"Aah! My hands . . ."

To encourage him, Aurel bounced again on the piano lid.

"Yes . . . Yes . . . Just let me go. Aah!"

"And you knew why he was calling you, didn't you?"

"Yes, I knew. Aah! My hands."

"And you didn't answer."

"No. Aah!"

"Jocelyne, search his pockets. See whether he has a weapon or not, and get his cell phone."

Hearing her name, Jocelyne came to. She had been gazing at the scene with horror and fascination. It had all happened so quickly, so unexpectedly, and was so brutal that it seemed unreal.

"His pockets," she mumbled, regaining her wits. "Yes. Okay."

She patted Cortegiani's shirt on his chest, under his arms, down his back, and around his waist.

"He's not armed."

"Well, well," said Aurel, somewhat disappointed. "I thought he would be. It's true he's not on duty now. And the telephone?"

"There's nothing on him."

"Go check his jacket. It's hanging in the entrance."

Jocelyne went to the door, rummaged through the jacket, and came back with a black smartphone in a very worn imitation leather case.

"Password?"

Cortegiani was focused on his pain. He was staying as still as possible to contain it. Any movement of his imprisoned fingers was excruciating. Aurel no longer needed to bounce heavily: the slightest twitch of his buttocks cut into the crushed finger bones and made his prisoner wail with pain.

"Password?" he said again.

"Scotch12."

"As simple as that! Not even a brand name?" laughed Aurel.

He switched on the phone and typed in the code. The screen appeared, with all its apps.

"There we go. You remembered to make Mayères's cell phone disappear, but you never thought someone might look at yours. Let's check the call list. It's really odd, but it's one of those things people never erase. Sometimes they really ought to . . . Here we are: the day of Mayères's death. Wow! Quite a few calls. Jocelyne, do you have Jacques's number? No, don't bother: I see his name among the contacts."

Then, turning to Cortegiani:

"Of course there was nothing secret about your acquaintance, because of Le Cercle."

Cortegiani was no longer reacting. Jocelyne wondered if the shock of what was happening had not caused his heart to fail.

"Aurel, be careful. He doesn't seem at all well."

"Who? Our customs officer? Oh, come on."

But he glanced at Cortegiani's face and saw that he was indeed displaying signs of distress.

"Okay, we'll let him go, since you're sticking up for him. In any case, he won't get far like this."

Aurel stood up and lifted the lid. Cortegiani removed his hands from the keyboard. They were all blue and distorted. The copper plate of the lock had cut the proximal phalanges at the base of his right hand, and they were bleeding.

Cortegiani raised his elbows and held his hands level with his face. He opened his eyes wide and began sobbing.

"Now," said Jocelyne, staring at Aurel, "you're going to give me an explanation."

"*We* are going to give you an explanation," he said, pouring himself a glass of wine.

He drank it avidly. During the entire operation, he had forced himself not to eat or drink anything, and now the tension was easing off slightly. He collapsed into an armchair and crossed his legs. Jocelyne was perched on the edge of the sofa. Cortegiani, slumped over on the piano stool, was still sobbing as he looked at his hands.

"I was wrong about your brother, believe me. I thought he was frightened. What a mistake! He was only frightened on that last day. And he begged for help from my music pupil here."

"Don't be cynical, Aurel."

"You're right. Forgive me."

He sat up in his armchair and leaned toward Jocelyne.

"Your brother was a hero, Madame. Or in any case, he wanted to be one. You yourself told me as much. I didn't pay close enough attention."

"It's our older brother who was a hero. Not Jacques, to my knowledge."

"Because he wasn't given the opportunity. Because he had to take over the family business; because he married a woman who made him work like a dog. But even that was proof of his willingness to be self-sacrificing."

"I'm well aware of that."

"Except that a martyr in business is not a martyr. Your older brother got a bullet in his helmet. Whereas in Jacques's case his only punishment was to make money. A great deal of money. More and more money. An ambitious person might find that fulfilling; it doesn't alleviate any desires for heroism."

"In that case, he should have changed his life much sooner. Why did he wait until he was sixty-five to start changing things?"

"He would have changed, I'm sure of that. But there was his daughter. Another ordeal. Another sacrifice. How to describe his behavior toward her? I read the letters he sent her. He stayed with her right to the end. And if you ask me, he was heroic."

"I suppose so."

Aurel raised his finger as if to object.

"Except! Except that it wasn't his struggle, it was his daughter's. He may have been heroic, but it was his daughter who died."

"You don't have to die to be a hero."

"No. But put yourself in his place. He fought, and he was incapable of saving his child. He was eventually full of incredible hatred toward the people who took her from him: her friends, other addicts, dealers. Dealers more than anything. So he thought, it's time to go to war for real. Like my brother. No more pretense—the company, the business world, all that; no more proxy fighting, hiding behind my daughter. I'm going there, and I'm joining up."

"Going where?"

"That's just the problem. In the world he'd lived in up to then, he couldn't have found a combat like the ones he wanted. As far as I know, he'd never had anything to do with drug dealers, big or small. And the little delinquents who were supplying his daughter would have been laughable targets, even supposing he knew where to find them. He had to go out into the world, aim farther and higher. That's when he thought of the boat."

"So you don't think he left to go sailing just to enjoy life, like he told his friends?"

"Did you buy all that? Remember, when we went to the marina, you said to me, 'How could he stand to be so idle?' He wasn't a man who dreamt of leisure or peace and quiet. He wasn't the type to let himself go soft, sitting under the coconut trees."

"So you think he came here with a precise goal in mind?"

"I don't know. Maybe he did some research into drug trafficking and the maritime routes. Maybe he heard about the marina's reputation by chance, on arrival. The fact remains that once he realized where he was, he stayed on and tried to get involved. That's when he met the individual here present."

Cortegiani was still motionless. He had placed his hands on his knees. He seemed to be crumpling in on himself, withdrawing from the world to forget his pain. Aurel called out to him:

"And now he's going to tell us what happened next."

Cortegiani gave a start, and grimaced.

"Your brother," continued Aurel, "increased the number of his contacts to try to find a useful interlocutor. It wasn't the boozers at the marina who could be of any use. So he joined Le Cercle and went to the Association of Merit meetings. A den of notables, including a lot of military men, police officers, and secret police."

Then, looking at the customs man:

"Did he come to you, or did you go to him?"

Cortegiani took a moment to realize he'd been asked a question.

"It was me."

"Of course, a pearl like that, you couldn't let it get away. How did it happen?"

Cortegiani made a face, as if the interrogation was disturbing him, focused as he was on his ravaged fingers.

"How did it happen?" shouted Aurel.

"He told Marcelly about his daughter . . ."

"Louder!"

"Mayères confided in Marcelly about the death of his daughter."

"And the old lawyer told you. He must act as your informant . . ."

"Kind of."

"So you approached this Mayères person . . ."

"First there was his lecture about the Algerian war."

"You were there?"

"Yes. His eyes shone when he spoke about how heroic the army had been, and his brother who'd been killed in action, and all that . . ."

"Okay, we get it. Piece of cake: it wasn't exactly hard for you to recruit him. He threw himself into the jaws of the lion."

"Precisely," said Cortegiani defensively. "And I don't see why I should take the blame . . ."

This brief burst of energy exhausted him. Again he curled in on himself, and a tear appeared in each eye.

"We're not blaming you for anything just now. We're listening. And then?"

Cortegiani let out an exasperated sigh. There was only one thing he wanted—to be left alone—but he could see that Aurel had no intention of letting him go.

"And then," he continued, his voice weaker, "we needed someone to watch the boats in the marina."

"Ravigot, the manager at the clubhouse, wasn't he already working for you?"

"Yes, but you can't see the whole marina from his terrace. And besides, at night he's drunk. He sleeps."

"Whereas I imagine Mayères was a good little soldier. Were you the one who told him to cut a porthole in the hull?"

"Yes.

"What for?"

"To keep an eye on the comings and goings in the marina."

"He had optics, cameras, microphones?"

"We gave him everything necessary."

"And he could keep watch at night, too?"

"He had infrared equipment."

"That's strange, we didn't find anything like that on the boat."

"I took it all away when I went on board after his death."

"What a surprise. And are you the one who took his phone, too?"

"I found it behind a locker at the foot of the mast, so . . ."

"So you tidied up. You don't like to see things lying around. I get it."

Aurel stood up, and Cortegiani flinched.

"Relax. I'm not going to hit you," said Aurel, laughing.

He went over to the red drape he'd hung on the wall and pulled it down. The two reconstitutions appeared: Mayères in his family spider web, and Mayères on his sailboat in the middle of the marina.

"Goodness, Aurel, you've really been working."

Jocelyne had stood up in turn, and, going closer to the wall, she peered at the papers Aurel had pinned there.

"Except you forgot me on the family diagram."

He became flustered, and blushed.

"I'm teasing you. Go on."

Returning to Cortegiani, Aurel regained all his self-confidence.

"And so, Mayères began to work for you, with all the little tools he had. The way I picture him, the reports he provided you with must have been flawless."

"Yes, he did good work.

"And you encouraged him. Since you had his file in hand, you knew how to cajole him. You talked to him about his daughter, how those bastards were flooding Europe with cocaine; you ordered books over the internet about the Algerian war and passed them on. That's how they operate," Aurel added, turning to Jocelyne. "That's how they pay the poor guys who go to the front for them. Plenty of fine words, but never a penny."

"He didn't need any pennies," Cortegiani protested feebly. "His safe was full of cash."

"Whether it was or not is not the issue. To you, these agents are just puppets, cattle. You figure out what they eat and give it to them. In any event, in the end, they're the ones who get eaten."

When he'd arrived in the West, Aurel had been briefly recruited by the French counterespionage services. They'd wanted to make him spy on the Romanian diaspora. He'd been able to study their methods at leisure. In the beginning, they'd only put moderate pressure on him, but he had quickly distanced himself from them, and then relations had soured. There had been threats, surveillance, blackmail over administrative documents. They only let him go once he got married and joined the diplomatic corps.

"And so that," he continued, "is how you uncovered the *Cork*?"

"Yes."

"Fill me in, I'm interested."

As the blood began to flow through his vessels again, Cortegiani's hands started to swell. His purplish skin was smooth and gleaming, expanding with the edema. His hands looked like boxing gloves. Cortegiani stared at them as if they didn't belong to him anymore.

"Fill you in?"

You could tell that speaking required a great deal of effort.

"Yes."

"Well, we'd been tipped off by the Americans. A sailboat called the *Sea Breeze* would be arriving from the Azores. And in Cartagena, the Colombians had filled the hold with five hundred kilos of cocaine. We were tracking it. When they get to Africa, they often transfer the cargo onto another boat to throw us off the scent."

Cortegiani spoke slowly. He had to drag the words out of himself. But every time he paused, Aurel trained his pitiless gaze on him, and he was frightened.

"It's rarely done on the open ocean because they're easy to spot, and we can board them. They prefer to operate in a port, at night. This time they chose the marina in Conakry because it's fairly discreet."

"So they transferred the drugs from the *Sea Breeze* onto the *Cork*?"

"Yes."

"And Mayères saw it all. And photographed it all."

"Yes."

"And then?"

"And then, you know."

"I want to hear it from you."

"We stuck a tag underneath the *Cork*, and when they reached international waters, we intercepted them and seized the shipment."

Cortegiani finished his sentence with a sigh, as if these final words had completely drained him of his last remaining strength. Jocelyne felt sorry for him, but Aurel didn't seem to have any intention of leaving it at that.

"Except that the *Cork* wasn't alone," he cried.

He turned to Jocelyne because this explanation was addressed to her.

"Drug traffickers are a wary lot, you know. They don't risk entrusting their merchandise to just anybody, in case one day a smuggler decides to make off with it. They always send one or more boats after them. To all appearances, these trackers have nothing to do with the boat they're watching. They travel separately, and their crews don't communicate. The boat being watched often doesn't even know who their 'guardian angel' is."

"I didn't know that."

"You didn't know. But he did. Didn't you, Cortegiani, you knew it well?"

"Yes."

"Your brother Jacques probably didn't know, either. But since he was a methodical man, he found out all on his own, didn't he, Cortegiani?"

"He did."

"Tell us about it."

Cortegiani moaned.

"It was nothing. He said he had some little clues that made him think there was a connection."

"A connection between the *Cork* and a South African sailboat called . . . called?"

"The *Good Hope.*"

"Very good," said Aurel ironically, patting the customs man on the shoulder.

That simple gesture brought a grimace to his face, because now both his arms were in pain.

"Allow me to sum up what happened next, my dear Jocelyne, so you'll understand where I'm headed. The traffickers lost a huge sum when the *Cork* was seized. They probably conducted their own investigation to figure out where their operation had been detected, and who by. I don't know how they went about it, but they soon found out who was to blame: the *Tlemcen*, and its solitary skipper."

"And they decided to eliminate him . . ."

"Not only eliminate him but also discourage anyone else from ever wanting to do the same thing again. The point was to kill him in such a spectacular way that it would serve as a lesson to anyone, near or far, who might be tempted to imitate him."

"Which is why they used the mast."

"Exactly."

Jocelyne and Aurel both turned and gazed at the wall, at Mayères's portrait.

"Poor Jacques," said his sister.

She suddenly seemed to realize that it was her brother who'd been treated in such a cruel, degrading way.

"Particularly as he had realized what was about to happen."

"You mean he knew they were going to kill him?"

Aurel pretended to bow to Cortegiani.

"That was when our friend here showed the world the grandeur of his soul. Didn't you, Cortegiani?"

And, turning back to Jocelyne:

"Yes, Jacques Mayères realized what was happening. When he saw the *Good Hope* sail into the marina, he had an immediate and very clear vision of what would come next."

"The boat could have just been passing back through the marina without intending to attack him," Jocelyne protested.

"It could have. You're right. But as soon as it arrived, Mayères understood that this wasn't the case. For a start, the *Good Hope* was on its own. It wasn't accompanying any other boat; all the boats in the marina had already been in Conakry for a long time. There was no logistical reason for it to stop, either. It had come from Dakar, which isn't far at all, so they didn't need any supplies, or water, or fuel. And then, look at the layout of the marina . . ."

He went up to the wall.

"Here you have the boats at anchor, all grouped together, and here you have Mayères. The *Good Hope* didn't anchor near the others. It stopped here, right by the *Tlemcen*. There was already something threatening about its position."

Aurel took a few steps back to assess the diagram he'd drawn on the wall and gazed at it, leaning back slightly like an art lover at a gallery opening, his glass of white wine in his hand.

"But above all, he knew the crew: he'd had plenty of time to observe them during their first stopover. He'd spied on them, photographed them, perhaps even listened to them, if our friends gave him a special microphone. He knew there were two people on board: a South African couple. They were the ones who had signed the harbormaster's register the first time through."

"But wasn't it the same crew this time?"

"It was. Only this time there were three of them. And the third man was a cause of great concern."

"Why?"

"Because he didn't seem to jibe with the usual appearance of the *Good Hope*. There are two types of people involved in this sort of trafficking, and our friends over at customs know that. You have the mafia, the Colombian gangs, the underworld of drug lords: they're hidden, they pull the strings. You never see them. And then there are the ones used to transport the goods, and they're the sort who look like butter wouldn't melt in their mouth. The crew of the *Good Hope* were exactly that: a nice little couple, sailing along the coast of Africa on their honeymoon."

"And the third man?"

"That's just it, he belonged to that other world, the violent world that's usually hidden. Except that this time, he wasn't on a smuggling mission, but something else."

Aurel took a long swallow of white wine.

"Something else indeed," he added, making a face, because the wine had gone warm in his hand. "An execution."

"Wait, let's get something clear: who was this third man?"

"I don't exactly know. Everything seems to imply he was a hit man sent on purpose by Colombian drug lords, someone from their ranks. A hired gun, in any case, with an Indian face, an athletic body, and nothing that predisposed him to play the role of attentive escort to a pair of newlyweds."

"How do you know all this?"

"Because our three protagonists called on a young Guinean man, a slight acquaintance of mine, to take their visitor ashore before the boat sailed. And in all probability, the visitor is the same man who came back after dark to borrow the same skiff that had taken him ashore. He waited for Mame Fatim and Seydou to leave, and then he went to carry out his evil deed."

"But since Jacques had his eye on them, he must have been on the alert."

"He should have been, but the girl had given him a sleeping tablet."

They looked at Mayères again, as if the fact of having understood what had happened to him might still save him.

"The poor guy must have been exhausted. The *Good Hope* had been there for two days, and he was constantly on the lookout. Watching them day and night. And he sought help. You counted them on Cortegiani's phone: at least thirty calls."

"But what did he want?"

"Hand me the phone, please. What was the code again? Ah yes. Scotch12. Let's see. With any luck, he hasn't erased the messages. I wonder if this gentleman didn't get a kick out of hearing this sort of call. Maybe he's keeping them so he can listen to them again. What do you say, Cortegiani?"

But the customs man, slumped on his seat, had stopped answering.

"Here. What did I tell you? The calls are here. Let's see."

Aurel turned on the loudspeaker and hit play. There was a busy signal.

"A pity. That one's empty. Poor Mayères must not have spoken every time. Let's try another."

Three wordless messages went by. Finally, in the fourth,

Jacques Mayères's voice rang out and filled the room. They all turned automatically to look at the photograph.

"It's me, Max. Again. I really need to talk to you. *Really*, you understand. They're up to no good. I have my eye on them, but I can't stay vigilant twenty-four hours a day. They've found me out. I'm sure of it. It's the same crew, from the time of the *Cork*."

"That's fairly explicit, don't you think?" said Aurel when the message ended. "Let's try another."

He searched and pressed play at random.

"The Indian is watching me through binoculars. He's been hiding in a cabin, but he opened a porthole, and I can see him. I don't know what to do, with my girlfriend here. As long as she's on board, I don't think they'll try anything. But tonight, I don't know. I don't want to put her in danger. Call me back, Max, please."

"Max. Is that you? How original you are at the customs office. One last one?"

Aurel started the voicemail again. It must indeed have been one of the very last messages. Mayères's voice was muffled, out of weariness, or perhaps because he was afraid he'd be overheard in the silence of the night.

"You didn't call me back, Max. I don't know what's going on, but I think I'm beginning to get it. It's true: I agreed to this mission, and I'll stick it out until the end. Let them attack, I'm ready. My gun is loaded. Before they get the better of me, I'll have time to do some damage. Goodbye, Max. Thank you. You gave me a good opportunity to settle scores."

The message was almost inaudible at the end. Jocelyne was crying. It was as if for just a moment Jacques Mayères was there among them—alive, dignified, doomed but, perhaps, happy.

"He was waiting for them . . . the poor man had no way of knowing that Mame Fatim thought she was doing the right thing, giving him a sleeping pill. In the end, there was no strug-gle."

Jocelyne wiped her tears and sat up straight.

"He said, 'I think I'm beginning to get it.' Get what? What is there to get?"

"Get why 'Max' never replied. He's going to tell you him-self."

Full of fear, Cortegiani saw Aurel coming toward him. He drew his hands away.

"He's going to tell us because he has nothing left to hide. We may as well hear his explanation, or at least his excuses. Don't you think, customs man?"

"I had no way around it."

"And what else?"

"As far as the Guineans were concerned, nothing had ever happened on their territory. If I admitted to having an agent in the marina, they would have lodged an official protest. Our accreditation is due to expire. Have you seen the uproar in the press? They're very touchy when it comes to their national sov-ereignty. They could very easily have refused to renew my authorization, or our colleagues'. Which meant our entire operation would have been brought down."

"You could have sent someone to help Jacques on his boat. Or to get him out for a few days, to hide him."

"Mayères'd been found out. Anyone we sent to help him would have ended up in the drug lords' sights, too. Once they identify someone, they don't let him go."

"In short, you didn't want to sacrifice another agent to save this one, who was done for."

"And the police?" said Jocelyne.

"That's a different administration," Cortegiani protested, with a sudden burst of dignity.

"Don't give me the excuse of the war between departments, please. How did you put it, the other evening, at Le Cercle?

Customs officers choose their cigarette from the pack . . . If you'd wanted to involve the police, you could've."

"And why didn't he?" asked Jocelyne, who was beginning to see the customs officer in a different light.

Compassion was gradually giving way to scorn and resentment.

"He won't tell you, but it's very simple. Terribly simple: he no longer needed your brother. Once an agent is unmasked, he's useless, even dangerous. It's better for him to disappear."

"And so what?" Cortegiani barked suddenly. "Yes, that's how it is, those are the rules of the game. You think we're dealing with choir boys in this business? We're fighting bastards who won't hesitate to kill. We do the dirty work. But it's necessary. Mayères understood that. He agreed to the contract, in full knowledge of the facts. You said so yourself: he was someone looking for a sacrifice."

"So you offered it to him. Out of the kindness of your heart!"

Aurel shrugged his shoulders. "No point in discussing this any longer. You have only your conscience to live with, and if you're at peace with it, well, good for you."

"What are you going to do?"

"Call Commissaire Dupertuis. And you're going to explain all this to him."

Cortegiani became sheepish. A shooting pain in his wound made him wince.

"And my hands?"

"I'll send for Dr. Poubeau. He's in house, one of us. He'll know to stay discreet, if we ask him to. And I don't think you want any publicity surrounding this business. Or am I wrong?"

XII

At five o'clock in the evening, the Conakry peninsula is saturated with color, and things seem more solid and solemn, ready for the drama of nightfall. The sea below the terrace where Aurel was sitting was veering Prussian blue, while to the south the sky was tinged a pinkish orange. Normally at this hour, Aurel should have been relaxing over a glass of chilled white wine to banish the heat of the day. But as he had just awoken from a deep sleep, he'd cautiously ordered tea and was trying to ingest a piece of sponge cake.

Jocelyne Mayères came up without a sound and startled him.

"What a night!" she said, sitting opposite him. "I was so upset I couldn't get to sleep before nine this morning."

The waiter came for her order, and she asked for a double espresso.

"Any news?"

"I had a message from Dr. Poubeau. He sent Cortegiani for X-rays. Five fractures of his phalanges, one of them open. He said he'd never seen the like from someone claiming to have jumped into an empty swimming pool . . ."

Aurel smiled with a grimace and blew on his tea.

"He doesn't believe it?"

"Whether he believes it or not, that's the version Cortegiani is sticking to, as he did last night with the commissaire. I think no one is fooled, but never mind."

"So you're off the hook?"

"You remember what Cortegiani said when he told the whole story to Dupertuis: nothing must get out. Officially, nothing happened."

"The poor commissaire: that's a lot to cope with in a single evening."

"You have to give him one thing: he knows how to own up to his mistakes. I spoke to him on the phone just now; in fact, he's the one who woke me up. He wasted no time."

The daylight was rapidly fading. The faint glow of lamps, lit here and there around the hotel terrace in preparation for nightfall, was beginning to stand out against the ultramarine background of the sky.

"He contacted Dakar, and it was easy to trace the *Good Hope*'s third crew member. He signed on under the name Ramon Alencar. It's a fake identity, naturally, but on the Interpol file, this matches one of the pseudonyms used by a certain Rigoberto Cortazar."

"Who's that?"

"According to the Interpol file, he's a member of the Cali cartel in Colombia. A fairly subordinate character, a sort of right-hand man for the network's godfather. But he was involved in several assassinations, and there's an international warrant out against him."

"Do we know where he is?"

"They've issued his description to the Guineans, but he's probably already long gone, in Guinea-Bissau or beyond."

"So we won't find him."

"No more than they found the man who put a bullet in your older brother's helmet."

"That's just what I was thinking."

Night had fallen. As always in this climate, Aurel thought the moment had come too quickly, and he experienced this darkening of things as an injustice, a punishment. Daytime, in this climate, never had the leisure to stretch out and laze about, to offer the endless summer evenings that are part of Europe's charm. Today, in particular, Aurel would have liked for the day, begun so late, to last a bit longer. It was the last day he'd be spending with Jocelyne, as she would be flying out at around midnight. He would have liked to have a few more images of her to keep, sunny and brightly colored. But instead, he had to be content with the faint flashes of her face he could discern in the near-darkness.

"And the South African couple on the *Good Hope*?"

"There's no evidence against them. Dupertuis suggested it would be better to let them go. They've been identified, now. Sooner or later they'll get caught during an operation. People like that always end badly. I took the liberty of telling him that I agreed."

"Dupertuis is asking you for your opinion! How extraordinary. When you think how angry he was when he arrived at your place last night and saw what you'd done."

"He's the pragmatic sort, and so is Cortegiani. They know that you're the one holding the cards. You've said you would drop the charges; if you change your mind, and, above all, if you tell the papers what you know, they're finished. The customs man's cell phone is still in our possession—I've got it carefully locked away in my safe. And as they've also realized that we're in this together . . ."

He felt an emotional catch in his throat on saying these last words.

"Still," said Jocelyne, "you were risking big. You were forced to—"

"To resort to what I did? Of course. A normal procedure wouldn't have gotten us anywhere with a character like Cortegiani. People like that are untouchable. The only way is to attack them on their own terrain. Which means being as violent and disloyal as they are."

Aurel let out a long sigh and rubbed his eyes. There was a

brief silence, then Jocelyne leaned forward and, to his surprise, took his hand.

"I wanted to say, Aurel . . . I don't know how, actually. The most ordinary thing would be just to say 'thank you.' But it goes deeper than that. Anyway, I am *truly* grateful to you."

Aurel shifted on his chair, looked into his empty cup. If only he had a glass of white wine in front of him . . . Jocelyne was still holding his hand. She was wearing a silver bracelet, and he watched as it trembled on her small wrist. This vision stirred an inexpressible emotion inside him.

"You're an extraordinary person, Aurel, really. It is a great honor to have met you."

What could he possibly say? Aurel felt his jaw drop, as if the nerves that controlled it had been brutally severed.

"We'll be saying goodbye in a little while," she continued. "I want you to know that I'll keep you in my heart, and that I know how much I owe you. And I hope you'll be happy. You deserve it."

At this level, kindness became cruelty. When she saw Aurel's eyes fill with tears, Jocelyne let go of his hand, and to allow him to regain his composure, she turned to a less personal subject.

"So Mame Fatim has been cleared? I hope they'll let her go."

"Dupertuis told the Guineans that we had found the culprit thanks to a tip from our secret services—not to have to go into detail and compromise the customs service. But it will take some time before Mame Fatim is released. The justice department will have to drop the charges against her. In the meantime, they'll probably offer to let her out on bail."

"I'll put up the money, if need be," Jocelyne said immediately.

"That's very generous of you. I'll keep you informed."

Aurel checked the time on his watch. In less than an hour,

they would have to leave for the airport. Jocelyne's flight was not until the middle of the night, but there would be a lot of procedures before that.

"In the end," she concluded, "the only one who won't be punished is that Lamine character. What's he going to do with that huge fortune? It's odd to think that all of Jacques's working life might go to creating some sinister underworld enterprise at the heart of Africa."

"I'm afraid your vision is a bit too romantic."

"Romantic!"

"Yes. In my opinion, your brother's destiny is much simpler, and nothing prevents us from seeing it as even more tragic."

"What do you mean?"

"That Lamine didn't steal his fortune."

Jocelyne gave a start. Aurel was so happy to provoke an emotion in her, no matter what kind, that he let the moment last.

"He stole *what was left* in the safe. Don't you remember, Mame Fatim told us it all fit into a little bag. Even if you have notes of five hundred euros, you can't fit tens of millions into a little bag."

"So what might Jacques have done with the rest?"

Aurel paused to smooth the tablecloth in front of him with the flat of his hands, as if he were trying to sweep away a welter of imaginary objects.

"We must forget everything we think we know and get back to Jacques's character. He was a man of conscience. After his daughter's death, he decided to go away and pursue, late in life, the same path as your heroic brother. But I'm sure he felt terribly guilty all the same."

"Toward whom?"

"Guilt doesn't need an object to exist. It's a feeling that comes from inside and takes root in a soil of emotion, memories, and desires that belongs to each one of us alone. Once it's fully grown, this plant fastens onto whatever it finds. That's my opinion, anyway."

Aurel was glad the darkness hid the blush on his brow. What had got into him, to come out with such a sermon? He went back to Mayères, to remove any impression he might've been speaking about himself.

"What drove Jacques—and I'm sure of this—was guilt. His guilt at not following your big brother's example; the guilt Aimée fueled in him for never giving her all she wanted; his guilt at not saving his daughter."

"And the guilt for leaving everything behind after Cléo's death. I would agree with you on that score. But what's your conclusion?"

"That he wanted to redeem himself. I'm convinced that when he left, he kept only what he needed for the bare necessities of his new life."

"And the rest of his fortune?"

"I think he left it to . . ."

"To who?"

"To Aimée."

There was a long moment of silence. Jocelyne had leaned back in her chair and disappeared out of the halo of lamplight, so Aurel could hardly make out her features. For a moment he began to dread her reaction. Jealousy, wounded pride, disappointment, greed, why not? What dark forces were at work inside her, and what violence might emerge? Fortunately, when she returned to the light, Aurel could see she had a huge grin on her face. Almost at once, she let out peals of laughter, liberating, banishing all the fumes of anxiety, the dark humors of regret and envy. Aurel hesitated for a moment, then began laughing in turn. Diners at the neighboring tables turned to stare at them. When their fit of laughter eventually subsided, Aurel had tears in his eyes.

* * *

The next morning, Aurel got to the consulate long before his department was due to open. He went up to his office with a gendarme who fiddled with a huge key ring to open the door for him.

He switched on the computer, launched the upload from the memory card he had just inserted, and ran to the shared printer in the corridor to switch it on. When the print-out appeared, he returned slowly to his office and pinned it on the wall. Then he copied the computer's hard disk to an external disk drive and waited. Not for long, either, because at eight o'clock, two agents from the maintenance department knocked on the door, as he had foreseen they would. They were rather embarrassed, but he put them at their ease.

"It was Monsieur le Consul Général who instructed us yesterday on his return . . ."

"Be my guests, gentlemen, go right ahead. It's all the same to me."

The two technicians unplugged the computer and all its connections, then put the machine on the cart they had brought with them and withdrew, pushing the cart ahead of them. A quarter of an hour later, Aurel picked up the telephone and pressed the key for an outside line. There was no dial tone: the line had been disconnected.

At around nine o'clock, Hassan knocked on the door. He seemed upset.

"The consul general's secretary was looking for you all day yesterday. He wanted to see you, urgently."

"All day, really?"

"Until early afternoon."

After that, Baudry must have spoken to the commissaire, who had filled him in. The condition for Jocelyne's silence about the affair was that no legal or administrative reprisals be brought against Aurel. All Baudry could do was put his colleague back in the closet where he'd been before these events. Which he did.

"And you were ordered not to work with me anymore and to go back to the mail desk?" he asked Hassan.

"How'd you know?"

"Do as they said, Hassan. I'm sincerely grateful to you for your help. You're a fine lad, full of merit."

Aurel stood up and held his hand out to the young man, and in the end, moved, they hugged each other.

When Hassan left the closet, Aurel sat back down, put a blank sheet of paper on his empty table, and went back to staring at the print-out he had tacked on the wall.

It was—Jocelyne had taught him the word—a *selfie* taken shortly before her departure the night before. In the picture, Jocelyne was smiling and Aurel was in two places at once. Because it was to him, the viewer, that she was smiling, but it was also Aurel, next to her, almost to cheek to cheek, who was grimacing painfully with happiness and farewell.

Aurel took a deep breath, uncapped his pen, and on hastily drawn horizontal lines that represented blank sheet music, he began to scrawl musical notes, humming all the while. The theme was very simple, scarcely four notes. They had come to him in the taxi from the airport like a revelation, but from this rich seed a great tree might grow, a forest. He could sense rhythm, variations, voices. He began composing, crossing out, pausing from time to time to reread it all, singing.

He had six months left to go in the closet in Conakry. Enough to write an entire opera.